THE TREE WITHIN

THE TREE WITHIN

The Answers Are On the Inside

Stephen Campana

RESOURCE *Publications* · Eugene, Oregon

THE TREE WITHIN
The Answers Are On the Inside

Resource Publications
An Imprint of Wipf and Stock Publishers
199 W. 8th Ave., Suite 3
Eugene, OR 97401

www.wipfandstock.com

PAPERBACK ISBN: 978-1-5326-5290-5
HARDCOVER ISBN: 978-1-5326-5291-2
EBOOK ISBN: 978-1-5326-5292-9

Manufactured in the U.S.A.   SEPTEMBER 13, 2018

Contents

PREFACE

KANYE WATCHED AS THE star, which he had been following for days, stopped and hovered in the night sky directly over the hospital, like a brilliant celestial marker. He knew what it was marking, too. The child was being born. Ancient prophetic fulfillment had not come far in the past two thousand years. Same old stuff. Dreams and visions, floating stars, "special" children being born. Some things never changed.

He tugged at the white bishop's collar around his neck. It was too tight, too cloying. These days it always felt too cloying. Surely that symbolized something, he thought.

He got out of the car and crossed the street. The Jersey City Medical Center stood like a colossus, reaching out into the night sky, its many buildings stretching east and west for almost half a mile. He had read somewhere that it was the largest hospital in the world, and he believed it. As he approached the entrance, the enormity of the task at hand began to jangle at his nerves, and he felt a thin layer of sweat forming on his black skin beneath the fabric of his uniform.

He pushed through the doors into the lobby. Off to the left, seated behind a glass pane, were two guards. He smiled and waved at them as he passed; they did not stop him. A bishop's uniform went a long way in a hospital. At the front desk he received directions to the maternity ward and proceeded toward the elevator. He got off on the fifth floor and followed the signs. The hospital was quiet as he made his way down the long, gray corridors. There was something about a hospital at night that was almost . . . peaceful.

Within moments he arrived at the nursery. He peeked in briefly at the newborns, gave them a wave, and then proceeded a few yards down the hallway to a waiting area, where he took a seat, crossed his legs, and waited.

He waited for hours and hours. Every so often he got up, checked the nursery, then sat back down and continued waiting.

It was not until the wee hours of the morning that he found what he had been waiting for, when a nurse brought a new baby into the nursery. Something told him that this was the one. But he did not check on it right away. Instead, he waited until the nurse came back out and the nursery was clear. Only then did he approach the window and look in. As he did, he saw a solitary figure in a nurse's uniform strolling slowly through the room, inspecting the newborns. She caught Kanye's gaze as she moved effortlessly about, and their eyes locked. Her lips twisted into a small, dark grin as she stopped at one of the cribs and grasped the rails. Then she raised her index finger, pointed it downward at the baby, and made a jabbing motion with it, as if to say *This is the one.*

Then the nurse's mouth curled into a grin that grew wider and wider, until the ends of her lips reached up to her temples. The rest of the face changed too, into a hellish visage the likes of which Kanye had seen only in horror movies. It opened its mouth to reveal three rows of razor sharp teeth, each about an inch long, with ropes of saliva dripping down from them, and onto the helpless baby in the crib below.

For a moment Kanye's hopes soared, as he thought the thing would just devour the baby right then and there, thus saving him the trouble.

But he would have no such luck; the thing soon changed back into a woman, then disappeared altogether, leaving behind only a thin mist of smoke. It had served its function. It had identified the child. The rest was up to him.

That was a responsibility he did not want, had never asked for, and still couldn't quite fathom. But the people he worked for insisted the cause was a just one, and that the fate of the world hung in the balance, so he had gone along. Who was he to question?

He went back to the waiting room and sat down. And continued waiting. A short while later a man appeared at the nursery window, peering in with wide eyes and a big smile.

Kanye approached him. "Which one is yours?" he asked. "That one right there," the man said, pointing at the one the thing had selected. "What a beautiful baby," Kanye said with his thick Ethiopian accent. "Why, thank you," the man said proudly.

Kanye stood and talked with the man for a good while, making sure to gain his affection and, more importantly, his trust, before asking "What's your name, sir?"

"Peter," the man said. "And your last name?" Kanye continued. "Landers," the man answered. "Is this for a mailing list?" he asked, upon noticing that Kanye was jotting his answers down on a small pad.

"Oh, no," Kanye replied with a polite chuckle. "You are going on my *prayer* list."

"I see," Peter smiled. "That's much better. I myself am a minister."

Kanye's eyes lit up. "Then you understand," he said, putting a hand on the new father's shoulder. "You see, Mr. Landers, this is a crazy world we live in. My faith tells me that to be born into this world is a blessing. But I wonder sometimes. Is it? I don't know. But I know this: Anyone coming into the world these days needs as much prayer as they can get. And I like to know who I'm praying for. When I remand a person to the Lord's care, I like to know who I'm remanding."

"I understand," Peter said, a note of appreciation in his voice.

Before the conversation was over Kanye had also gotten his address. It wasn't difficult. A bishop's uniform was an instant trust grabber.

Kanye said his good byes, took a last look at the baby, and went on his way. Of course, he would not simply take the man's word for it; he checked it out with his sources and found that Peter had indeed provided him with reliable information. That was good. It was a start. The hard part, of course, was still to come.

Killing the child.

ACKNOWLEDGMENTS

THE INSPIRATION FOR THIS book derived from an essay by Jacob Israel called "Garden of Eden Revealed!". The ideas have been used with permission.

PART 1

SILVERTON

1

JACK HORN WAS THE last one on the bus. He figured he might as well take it all the way to the terminal, since he didn't know where he was anyhow. Except for the name of the town and the state. Silverton, Illinois. The important thing was: he had put enough distance between himself and his last place of residence to throw the hounds off his trail for a little while.

He got up from his seat in the back and moved up to the front, seating himself near the exit. He put his back pack on the seat next to him and stretched out his legs, folding them at the ankles. He just sat there like that, relaxing, for the next ten minutes, until the bus finally arrived at the terminal.

As it crawled to a stop, he stood up and strapped on his back pack.

"Have a nice day, chief" he said to the driver, and got off the bus. "You too, son," the driver replied. Jack looked around. The terminal was mostly empty. More empty buses than people. He headed for the exit, which led into a rather busy part of town. He walked some ways, until he arrived at an intersection in what appeared to be the center of town—a small town by the looks of it. He pondered his choices, then turned right onto a street called Main, and found himself passing by a long line of shops, pizza parlors, saloons, and diners. It was the last one on that list that he wanted right now, as he hadn't eaten for hours.

He ducked into a place called The Diner Train. It was a small place, dimly lit, with a counter up front, tables in the middle, and booths on the sides by the windows. The diner was mostly empty, which made sense, as it was the middle of the afternoon. A guy in a construction uniform sat hunched over at the counter, picking at a slice of pie; at one table sat a mom and her small child, munching on French fries, and at another sat an old couple nursing two coffees.

Jack took a window seat in one of the booths. While he waited, he looked outside, trying to get a feel for the town that was probably going to be his new home for a while. Not that it mattered much. Wherever he went, people were the same. And it was still the same you. Can't get away from that. Like the saying went: *Wherever you go, there you are.*

A waitress came over with a menu. She was a short girl, heavy set, with a bright smile and perky breasts that spilled halfway out of her low-cut blouse. "Do you need some time to decide?" she asked, handing him a menu. "Yes, please," Jack said, taking it from her. "Be back in a few," she chirped. Jack traced the subtle gyrations of her posterior as she sauntered off. If life on the road had taught him anything, it was that you had to take time to enjoy the simple pleasures. You never know what tomorrow will bring.

Jack perused the menu. With eleven dollars to his name, there weren't a lot of choices. He decided to go with the burger and fries. When the waitress returned moments later, he placed his order and said "Hey, I was hoping you could help me with something."

"I will if I can," she said.

"I'm kind of new in town, and I'm looking for work. Any advice?"

"If you need work, and you need it like, right now, your best bet is Manus Manufacturing. It's a big place, they're always hiring, and they take anyone. My brother used to work there until he got fired for being late too much."

"Sounds good, where is it?" Jack asked.

"Old Hook road."

"How do I get there?"

The waitress pointed out the window as she spoke, saying "Go straight down this block, till you pass the railroad tracks. That's old Hook Road. Make a left and go up about two blocks."

"Great," Jack said. "You've been a big help."

"I hope so," she smiled. "Be right back with your burger."

About ten minutes later she returned with his meal. He gobbled it down quickly, then made his way out, and headed down the street to what he hoped would be his new place of employment.

⟿

Her directions were right on the mark. There it was, right where she said it would be—Manus Manufacturing—a long, narrow building, three stories high, with rows of windows running across each level, and a smoke stack on the roof that was belching forth a steady cloud of thick, black fumes. He strolled through the mostly full parking lot toward the entrance, and pushed through the large glass double doors, into the lobby of the plant. In front of him was a long counter with a glass pane over it, and little slots in the glass every few yards or so. Above the slots were holes that you could talk through.

He positioned himself by one of the holes and waited for someone to notice him. Behind the glass several workers, mostly women, shuffled about busily. After several long moments, an elderly woman wearing thick glasses attached to a lanyard approached the window and said in a distant voice "Can I help you?"

"I'd like to apply for a job," Jack said. The woman turned away, walked over to the back wall, and took a paper off a large pile of them. Then she came back and slipped it through the slot, saying "Fill this out. When you're finished, Mr. Hall will speak to you. He's does all the hiring around here." *The guy who does the hiring,* Jack thought. *Perfect. That's the man I want to see.*

He took the application over to a table off to the left of the entrance, filled it out, and approached the window to return it. This time a different woman came over, also older, but with a decidedly nicer disposition. She took the application from him, paged through it very quickly, then said "Bring this up to the second floor, to Mr. Hall's office." Then she smiled and said, "Good luck."

"Thank you," Jack replied, and headed for the elevator. He pressed 2, waited for a moment, and got out. Application in hand, he walked down a narrow, musty corridor, and knocked on the door with the words *Ed Hall: Hiring Manager* on them. "Come in," a gravelly voice rasped from the other side of the door.

He entered. Off to his right sat a fat, balding man behind a desk. He was in his late forties to mid-fifties, and he had a harried, nervous look about him. His face glistened with a thin layer of sweat. He wore a white shirt with the sleeves rolled up and suspenders. Jack wasn't sure he had ever seen a person wearing suspenders outside of the movies. On the desk was an ashtray filled with crushed cigarette butts. That explained the raspy voice. Did people still smoke in offices these days? Did people still smoke at *all* these days? Another blast from the past. Maybe this guy had been teleported in from the nineteenth century.

"How are you?" the man asked, extending a hand across the desk. "Very well, thank you," Jack replied. He shook Hall's hand and sat down, then handed him his application. Hall slid his glasses down from the top of his head and studied it, his face blank. When he was finished he smacked the application with his hand, fingers spread, as if trying to hold it in place against a strong wind and stared intently at Jack. He slid his glasses back up, then said "You don't stay at your jobs very long. Lots of moving around."

Jack could not argue with that. The man would have to be blind not to notice that he had done a lot of hopping around. "That's true," Jack said. He was not about to offer any explanations or excuses. This was the kind of job you got because you couldn't find anything better. If he had a good resume, an impressive portfolio, or any meaningful skills, he would not be there in the first place.

Undeterred by Jack's reticence, Hall placed his glasses back on and began reading items off the application. "Bestfoods Vending, two months; Conway Packing, five months; Monte's Meat Plant, four months." He paused and scratched his head. "And they're all in different towns. Akron. Ashford. Cedar Lake." He looked at Jack intently, concerned almost. "Why do you move around so much, son?"

Again, Jack wasn't biting. "I guess I'm just one of those restless souls," he smiled. "Real restless," Hall agreed. "Don't you have any family?"

"Sure," Jack said, "But I'm kind of on my own now. They're in Oklahoma."

Hall just stared blankly into space for a second, then got up, pounded the desk, and said "Follow me."

Jack followed Hall out into the hallway, onto the elevator, where the hiring manager pressed the number 3. Moments later the doors opened into a large factory area. It was hot as hell and bustling with people. Rows of conveyer belts shuttled merchandise from one person to the next, with each person performing a different task—counting, pressing, packaging, and finally, stacking, until the merchandise was neatly arranged on pallets and ready to be taken out to trucks, which were parked, backs open, at various bays throughout the floor. "Well, this is it," Hall said. "Think you could handle this for eight hours a day?"

"I think so," Jack said.

"Good, you're hired," Hall replied. "Be here tomorrow at nine and we'll get you started. Pay is nine bucks an hour; benefits kick in after 90 days, if you stick around that long."

"Thank you," Jack said.

Mr. Hall wandered off on the floor while Jack got back on the elevator and took it down to the lobby. He had gotten his job. Whoopee! In a week, he could afford to rent a room. Buy some food. Scratch out a meager existence in this two-horse town until they caught his scent, and he had to flee again and start all over someplace else. They say to be grateful for small blessings, but he did not feel grateful for this one, or, truth be told, for anything in his life. He never wanted any of this. Who would? Being hunted like a crocodile, forced to flee from town to town, never allowed the chance to make friends or establish relationships. And all in the service of a mission that he did not want, did not understand, and, he suspected, probably could never fulfill. Why him? Why couldn't God have chosen someone else to lead the human race back to the Garden of Eden?

2

WELL, AT LEAST I'VE got a job, Jack thought as he rinsed and spat in the sink of the bathroom at the Silverton Public Park. *A couple of paychecks and I'll get a room somewhere.*

In the meantime, he was homeless. Not *hardcore* homeless, living in alleys, eating out of the trash, and pushing around a wagon full of empty cans. This was more of a temporary, between homes homelessness.

He put the toothbrush back in a baggie, along with his comb and a razor blade, tossed them in his backpack, and left the bathroom. He walked down a narrow, gravelly path, past some tennis courts, and over to a cluster of park benches which surrounded some picnic tables. He placed the back pack on the table, unzipped it, and pulled out a blanket. Then he brought the blanket over to the bench, kicked off his shoes, and laid down, face up, on the bench.

The night sky was full of stars. He started counting them. It was something he did to help him sleep—a trick his dad had taught him on the camping trips they used to take together when he was a kid. Back when he used to have a real life. As he lay there, he heard a strange, low-pitched rumbling. Without getting up, he looked around, cutting his eyes this way and that. He heard it again. It was coming from under the picnic table. It was a cat. Growling softly, the creature approached him, then stopped, midway between the table and the bench, pondering whether or not to proceed further. Jack put a hand on the concrete and tapped, encouraging the feline to come forward. Slowly, and with great deliberation, it did. Jack stroked it. It purred. Slowly, trust was established, and the cat climbed into the bench with Jack, curling itself into a ball in his chest. Cuddling the cat like a pil-low, Jack's breathing slowed, his eyes grew heavy, and his body grew cooler. Soon both he and the cat were fast asleep.

3

PETER LANDERS SORTED THROUGH the mail, tossed most of it to the side, and held up one piece—a letter, postmarked Akron, Ohio. "We got something from Adam," he called out to his wife. He didn't call him Jack or any of the other surnames he had taken over the years as he wandered the country trying to throw his assassins off his trail. He called him by his birth name—Adam. That's who he was and always would be, no matter what. His son—Adam. His wife came running in from the kitchen and snatched the envelope from Peter's hand. They sat together on the sofa as she opened it up. She read it aloud:

> *Hi, folks. Doing okay. I'm still in Akron. Working at a packing plant. Boring work, but it pays for the room I'm renting. I think they've got my scent again, though; I guess I'll be leaving soon. I will keep you posted. Love you both.*

She put the card down on the coffee table and stared at Peter. She said nothing. She didn't have to. He knew what she was thinking. They had been through it all a thousand times. They would love to have him there with them, but that wasn't working out. As long as he was there, they would have to keep moving, as they did for the first eighteen years of his life. And it was just a lot easier for one person to run than for a whole family. So, Adam, against their wishes, ran. And he'd been running ever since. But wherever he ran, no matter how fast or how far, he was still their son. And nothing could change that.

4

JACK FOLLOWED SLOWLY BEHIND as Mr. Hall lead the way along the long, wide perimeter of the factory floor, which was a maze of conveyer belts, stacks of merchandise, and pallet jacks. In place of air conditioning, the massive room was cooled by fans, placed strategically throughout the floor. Even so, it was sweltering. Every so often Hall would stop, point something out, then continue the tour. He finished by handing him off to another worker, who he instructed to show Jack the ropes. He was an older fellow, about sixty, with a slight paunch, big beefy arms, and a patch over one eye. "I'll take it from here," he assured Hall as the office manager thanked him and scuttled off to attend to other business.

The two men stood side by side behind a conveyer belt, one in five rows of such belts that took up most of the factory floor. Behind each belt stood four workers, spaced about three yards apart, with each one performing a particular task to prepare an item for shipment. The items in question were filters, the kind used in AC and furnace vents. Jack's job, it appeared, would be to take two filters, place them on top of each other, then pass them down the line. The old man, next in line, would put a press on them from an overhead hanger, then move them down to the next person. At any rate, that's how the older gentleman explained it, and it worked for Jack. He began slinging the filters down the line. As he worked, every so often, the older gentleman would offer a brief instruction, correction, or just a thumbs up sign. After an hour or so, the man said: "Not exactly exciting work, is it?"

"Not really," Jack smiled, wiping the sweat from his brow "But it pays the bills."

"That's about the size of it," the man said. "By the way, my name's Kurt."

"I'm Jack," Jack replied.

"So, Jack," Kurt asked, eying him curiously, "How's a guy like you wind up at a place like this?"

The question did not offend Jack. There was no trace of judgment in Kurt's voice. "Well, it's like this," Jack said, and proceeded to tell the man the absolute truth. He told him about the attempts on his life growing up, how he left home to protect his family, how he moved from town to town to keep a step ahead of the assassins, and how he had been chosen to lead the world back to the garden of Eden. When he was finished, Kurt just stared at him curiously for several moments, then threw his head back and let out a big, hearty laugh. "Oh, that's good!" he said, waving a finger at Jack. "That's really good. You should write that down. Might make a good book."

"Ya think?" Jack asked, passing down some more filters. "Oh, yeah," Kurt said, still chuckling. "That's some good stuff. You've got a good imagination, kid."

"Thank you," Jack said. He could tell by the man's cadence, his enunciation, and just his general *presence* that he was an intelligent person. In fact, he might have asked the man the same question he had just asked him, because he knew this man was capable of much greater things than slinging filters down a conveyer belt. He thought about asking but decided not to. There would be plenty of time for that. For now, he would just keep his mouth shut and do his job. Which is exactly what he did for the next two hours, until he saw something that changed everything. *Someone*, actually.

She was three rows up, standing at the second slot on the first conveyer built. She had turned to say something to the person next to her, so he caught only a side glance, but he thought it was her, and suddenly, a wave of exhilaration swept through him with such force that he had to lean up against the conveyor belt to keep from falling. It wasn't just exhilaration; it was something he had not felt much of in a long time—hope. A hope that this girl, whom he had seen in his dreams every day since puberty, whom he thought, most likely, was a figment of his imagination, a carrot on a stick that he would never touch, was, in fact, real. He steadied himself against the conveyor belt and took a deep breath. He had to know, and he had to know now. He looked at Kurt and said "I need a drink of water. I'll be right back."

"No hurry," Kurt replied amicably.

Jack made his way down the side of the factory floor, past all the conveyor belts, up to the front of the room, where he got himself a drink. As he slurped up the water flowing up from the fountain, he could feel his heart racing with fearful anticipation. What if it *wasn't* her? Well, if it wasn't her, then it wasn't her; it would only serve to further confirm what he already suspected: God liked to play cruel jokes. He was a sick, sadistic prick. But if it *was* her? Well, then suddenly his world, gray and closed and suffocating, would open up like a flower greeting a fresh ray of sunlight. He took a deep breath, marshaled his courage, and turned around for a good look.

It was her.

With his head in the clouds, he went back to his station, and resumed his duties. For a few moments, he actually felt like he could float, and at one point he felt his feet leaving the ground and had to look down to make sure he was still fastened to the earth. He was. But nothing would be the same again now that he had seen her in the flesh—the girl who was supposed to help him lead humanity back to the garden of Eden. Eve.

5

As Jack made the trek back from work to the place that served as his un-official and temporary residence, the Silverton Public Park, he felt a kind of giddy schoolboy euphoria that he had not experienced in . . . well . . . ever. Oh, he had experienced the usual crushes, the cases of puppy love, the teen-age trysts, and even one or two torrid affairs, but nothing like this. This was something different. This was *spiritual.* Literally. He knew this girl—Eve—in the realm of spirit. He only just now could admit that to himself. Until today, when he saw her face to face, he had told himself she was just a dream, albeit a recurring one, and one that involved depths of sensation and emotion a hundred times more powerful than anything a person could experience in real life.

He sat down at the park bench, unzipped his back pack, and pulled out several bags of chips and pretzels that he had pilfered from the break room at work. When you had no home and no money, you learned little tricks to survive. One of the first he had learned was never pay for something you could get for free. And in a large factory you could almost always find unclaimed food lying around in the break room. Discarded potato chips may not be anyone's idea of a culinary delight, but it could get you through some tough times. It was called stretching the soup, and he had become a master at it. Then again, necessity was the mother of invention. Not many people could live the way he did. *He* couldn't live the way he did when he first started. But he learned fast. He had to.

He ate half a bag of chips and saved the rest. That was another trick he had learned. Eat only as much as you need to. The body could go a long time with very little food, as any holocaust survivor could attest. You really only needed water to survive, and he had all of that he needed. He had taken three bottles of water from the break room fridge, and should he run out, which, in this heat he just might, there was always the park sinks and water fountain. It was not high living, but it was enough to get by. And getting by was what he was all about. Unfortunately.

He strolled around the park as the day wore on, taking in the sights—the tennis courts, the fountain in the center of the park, the memorial to the park's founder, Dr. Winston Hibbard, the botchy ball court, and a number of ball fields: two soccer, three baseball, and one football. It was a big park for such a small town. As the day slowly turned into night, and the oppressive heat faded mercifully away, he made his way back to the picnic area, and prepared to sleep. It was hard to sleep outside; the body had to be cool to slumber, but the exhaustion he felt from the day's work would help. It would take some time—perhaps hours—but eventually his body would cool down, then shut down.

He retrieved his blanket, and lay down on the bench, face up. He tried counting the stars, but it didn't work. He was too fired up from work, from the heat, from seeing *her*. He closed his eyes, took deep, slow breaths, and tried to force all thoughts from his mind. It took some time, but he began to feel drowsy. Even so, he did not fall asleep right away.

After about half an hour he heard a feint, low-pitched growl. He looked around. It was the cat again, staring at him cautiously from under the picnic table. It had returned. Just as he did last night, Jack put a hand on the concrete and tapped, encouraging the cat to come to him. And just like last night, it did, only this time with less hesitation. The cat was starting to trust him now. It hopped onto the bench and snuggled against Jack's chest. Jack held it tight, like a pillow, as his breathing slowed, and his body temperature dropped. Soon both he and the cat were fast asleep.

Soon after that the dream started. Jack had the sensation of being under a pool of warm, messaging water, but he wasn't. When he opened his eyes, he could see he was chest deep in a pool of red rose petals. They were all around him, as far as his eyes could see—an ocean, fanning out in all directions. A bright blue canopy of cloudless sky stretched above him, and midway between the sky and the rose petals, were branches filled with lush green leaves dipping down from towering trees and terminating only several feet above the pool of flowers. It was like a scene out a Picasso or a Rembrandt painting. If there was a heaven, he thought, it could not be much better than this. The motion of the petals on his naked body felt like the massage of a thousand soft, supple hands. But apart from that motion, he felt another one. The motion of something else in the pool of petals moving toward him.

And then, in the distance, he saw her, gliding slowly, almost floating, through the petals, her body submerged, but her head and neck visible, and her arms outstretched, lightly touching the surface of the pool of petals as she floated forward, heading straight toward him.

She stopped right in front of him. Then she slid one hand around his neck and dipped the other into the petals, where she brought it to rest on his stomach, palm flat against his skin. She began moving it in circles, slowly, and with great care and precision, as if performing the most intricate of procedures. The warmth of her hand radiated through his body, her touch almost too wonderful to endure. Slowly she drew his face closer to hers as she moved her other hand up toward his chest. The circles grew harder and faster, covering the length of his entire upper torso. Waves of electricity passed through her hand into his body, and his muscles began to melt with a pleasure beyond imagining. As she drew his lips closer to hers, he could feel the warmth of her breath on his face, and when their lips touched he felt like he was literally about to melt into her, and she into him, and he wanted it to happen; he wanted to be sucked into her all the way, until they became as one, intertwined body, spirit, and soul. But then she withdrew, pushing him back, gently. Then she turned her head back and forth in a gesture that said *no*. And when he reached for her again, she was gone. Diane was gone.

When Jack woke up, the cat was still cradled in his arms. He had slept well. He felt refreshed. He got up and walked over to the picnic table, where he had left his back pack. The cat woke up, stretched itself, and sidled up beside him, rubbing itself against his leg, as he retrieved some toiletries from his bag. He took a few chips from the bag, and fed them to the cat, who purred gratefully.

Then he went to the bathroom, with the cat following. He peed, washed up, brushed his teeth, then headed back to the picnic table. He put his back pack on and set off for work. The cat followed for about twenty yards, then stopped, leaving him to go the rest of the way by himself. Jack hoped he would see the cat again tonight. He liked the feel of it against his bosom as he lay on the bench. They were just two strays who had found each other. Brought together by circumstances. He would have to give it a name and, eventually, a home. But first things first. And the first order of business now was to get to work and meet the girl of his dreams.

6

Kanye Balewa pulled his red Ford Sedan into the parking lot of the Red Robin motel off of route 9 in the town of Silverton, Illinois. It was a small motel, just one level, comprised of a row of about ten rooms, with an adjoining office off to the left. He got out of the car, retrieved a suitcase from the trunk, and went into the office. Behind the counter stood a studious looking young man with thinning hair and bifocals. The man said in a friendly voice "Hello sir, can I help you?"

"I need a room," Kanye said, smiling. His pearly white teeth were a stark contrast with his black face. "Right away, sir," the man said. He had Kanye sign in and pay, then he grabbed a key from a wall with a set of keys on it, each one on its own separate hook. "You'll be in room ten," he said, handing Kanye the key. Kanye took the key, left the office, and strolled down the row of rooms until he reached the last one—number ten. He let himself in.

It was a nice enough room: a bed opposite a dresser with a TV on it, a desk in the corner with a mini-fridge next to it, two nightstands on either side of the bed, and a closet just off the entrance. The bathroom was next to the closet. He put his suitcase on the bed and unzipped it. He took out some toiletries, and put them in the bathroom, then zipped up the suitcase, and put it in the closet. Then he kicked off his shoes, and laid down on the bed, his head propped up against the headboard.

This was not where he wanted to be right now. It was not what he wanted to be doing with his life. He was not a killer; he was a priest. But what did that even mean anymore? Did it ever mean anything? At first it did. He *was* a priest, a *real* priest at first. He knew who He was serving, and he was proud to serve Him.

And then, slowly, things began to change. The secret meetings, the private instructions, the things whispered in the dark by people who, officially, did not exist, about things that, officially, were not even real. But even through all of that he thought he knew whose side he was on. And even after he was told to kill Adam—even then he still believed he was serving God, and that his mission was to kill the anti-Christ. He was so blind! He realized now that's why they chose him. They wanted someone they could fool, someone blinded by their ideals, someone so zealous for good, so committed to the church, and all it stood for, that they would not ask questions; they would not doubt.

But the doubt crept in. *Gradually*. That was the key word. The unseemly things of a religion—any religion—were revealed gradually, and only to a few. And by the time those few knew the truth, they were a part of the lie; they were invested in it; complicit, and that made it hard to back out, or to even *want* to back out, for that meant incurring the wrath of a system they could not possibly defeat, along with giving up their livelihood. It was easier just to believe what they told you and go along with the program.

But he knew. He knew who he was serving, who the entire Christian church was serving. At best, it was a thinly veiled secret among the church hierarchy, although those on the lower rungs would be shocked to know.

7

JACK SAID GOOD BYE to the cat and started making his way down the narrow gravel path that lead to Main Street. The cat followed him for the first few yards, then stopped, sat down, and watched him go. He hoped it would still be there when he got back. He had grown fond of the little critter.

He turned onto Main Street and continued his trek, his mind a restless pool of nervous anticipation. Main Street was coming alive; the streets were filling with cars, the sidewalks with pedestrians shuffling along to their appointed tasks; merchants were busy opening shop, unlocking the doors, putting the *open* signs in the windows, preparing for the morning onslaught. Here and there people passed with their dogs, sniffing around at the end of their leashes for the best place to relieve themselves. A middle-aged woman with a Scottish Terrier gave him a big smile as the creature pulled her along the sidewalk. He smiled back. He had a lot to smile about today.

He crossed the railroad tracks onto Old Hook Road, made a left, and stopped at the sprawling edifice that was Manus Manufacturing. He checked his watch. Three minutes to nine. Right on time, if he hurried. He didn't want to be late for his second day at work. He walked briskly through the lot, through the doors, and to the elevator. He pressed 3, waited, then got off, heading straight for the punch clock. He made it by seconds. He dumped off his back pack in the locker area and arrived at his station at about one minute after nine. Kurt was already there, a slight smile on his face. He took his place next to the older man and took up where he left off yesterday, slinging filters onto the conveyor belt. "Congratulations," Kurt said, "You made it to your second day. A lot of people don't."

"It's not that bad," Jack replied. "Just boring and hot." As he spoke, he was looking several rows up, at the spot she had been yesterday. She had not arrived yet. "Yep," Kurt said. "Boring and hot."

For the next half hour, he made small talk with Kurt. He learned that Kurt had spent ten years in the merchant marine, then another thirty as a truck driver, until he lost his eye in a boating accident and had to retire. That, and a run of bad luck and some health issues, is how he ultimately wound up working in a sweat shop in a two-horse town for nine bucks an hour. Kurt finished his story by saying "It's not as good as *your* story, but it is what it is", to which Jack laughed heartily, and said nothing.

By that time, he was getting nervous. Eve had still not arrived. He had begun to wonder if perhaps she had quit. Maybe he just happened to catch her on her last day and would never see her again. Except, of course, in his dreams. The thought made his heart sink. Or what if she had gone on vacation? How would he even know? He didn't know her name; he couldn't ask anyone about her. Maybe he would have to come here every day for the next week or two, stand there all day slinging filters, and wait for her to return from Cancun or the Caribbean or wherever else she might be.

And then another thought, equally horrible, occurred to him. What if she had a boyfriend? Or a husband? She was pretty, and usually pretty girls did have boyfriends or husbands. How could it be that this hadn't occurred to him? Because he was *drunk,* that's why! Drunk with this stupid, childish idea that he had just discovered the woman of his dreams—*literally*—and that he and this woman were destined to go on a great journey together. Other than the voices in his head, some dumb-assed dreams, and a psycho who was always trying to kill him, what reason did he have for believing any of that? None. None at all.

And yet he did believe it. At least he thought he did. One thing he *did* know: he knew this girl. In his dreams, they made a deep connection—a connection of body, mind, and soul. He knew her, and he loved her. And now that he knew she actually existed he could not imagine the hurt he would feel to find out that she might never love him back. If that were so, he thought that maybe he would just stop running and let himself be killed. There would be no reason to go on.

"You all right there, kid?" Kurt asked. "You seem to be kind of zoning out." Jack smiled, embarrassed. "Oh . . . Yeah. I guess I'm just a little tired. Didn't sleep too well last night."

"That'll do it," Kurt said, "There's no substitute for a good night's rest. I remember when . . ."

Jack did not hear the rest of the man's words, because at that very moment, he saw her. She passed right by him, on his right-hand side, walking quickly, and turned down the corridor that lead to the locker rooms. She was there. And suddenly all the heaviness lifted and all of the hope returned. She was there, not in Cancun or the Caribbean, or anywhere else. She was there, at Manus Manufacturing, on 66 Old Hook Road in Silverton, Illinois. And he would, at some point, have the chance to talk to her. The thought at once terrified and exhilarated him. Did she know him the way he knew her? Had she dreamt about him? What if she knew nothing about him, about their mission? What if she didn't want to know anything about it? What if he told her and she just looked at him as if he were crazy? And what if she had a boyfriend or a husband?

Too many what-ifs. He was driving himself crazy. Maybe if he found out something. Anything. He waited for her to return from the locker room, which she did moments later. She walked over to her station, exchanging a few pleasantries with the woman next to her, and commenced work. Her job was to take the finished, fully boxed filters and place them next to her on a pallet. She worked with a kind of calm, rhythmic ease.

"So," Jack asked, "What's the story with that one? The first one on the first belt up there." He pointed. Kurt smiled at him. "Oh, you mean Diane?" he said. "Yeah," Jack said, trying to sound matter-of-fact. "She got a boyfriend? Husband?" As he waited for Kurt's reply, he could actually feel his heart suddenly accelerate to what must have been about a hundred and thirty beats a minute. So much hinged on his answer to that question. Too much. He didn't like to feel so helpless. "Definitely no husband," Kurt said, then stopped and thought for a moment before continuing: "And . . . I don't think she's got a boyfriend either. Nope, I think the path is clear." He gave Jack a smile. For the second time that morning, Jack felt a wave of relief. But he also felt a bit wobbly. The excitement, along with the heat, was getting to him. He turned to Kurt and said "I'm gonna take a five."

"Make it a ten, no hurry," Kurt replied, giving him a thumbs up sign.

Jack went to the break room. It was an average sized room, with three long rectangular tables in a row. Off to one side of the tables were two vending machines—one for soda, one for snacks—and off to the other a table with a coffee machine on it. On the wall opposite the tables was a sink, some counter space, and a refrigerator. Behind the tables were lockers. The room was empty except for an older woman seated in the corner of the room poking at a salad in a small Tupperware dish. Along with the salad she had a fruit drink, a small bag of pretzels, and another Tupperware dish full of what looked to be some kind of condiment or dressing. Mercifully, the room was about twenty degrees cooler than the factory floor.

Jack rummaged through some cupboards, looking for cups. He found one, went over to the sink, and poured himself some water. Then he took a seat at the middle table, on the end, back facing the door. He took a sip of the water and glanced briefly at the woman. She had long scraggly black hair, a large, crooked nose, and she looked either very bored, very tired, or both. Around her shoulders was a thin, finely woven black shawl. She looked at him and said, "Is this your first day?"

"Second," Jack replied. He took another sip of water. He was feeling better already. The woman nodded, as if his answer had somehow explained something important. "Yeah, it takes some getting used to," she said. "Yeah," Jack agreed. "Especially the heat."

"Oh, that's the worse," the woman said. "Sometimes I feel like I'm gonna feint."

"I believe it," Jack said. "How long have you been working here?"

The woman looked up at the ceiling, her face a mask of intense thought, as she tried to recollect the correct answer to his question. "Well, I started in 89 . . . So, I guess about . . . twenty-eight years."

"Wow, that's a long time," Jack said.

"Too long," the woman said, then went back to her salad.

Jack didn't know how to respond to that, and the two said nothing more. A few moments later someone else came in the room and said, "Hey Donna!", then went to her locker and opened it. Jack's heart leapt in his chest as he watched the girl rifling through her locker. It was her. It was Eve. And when she was done rifling through her locker, she came right over to his table, a bag of potato chips in her hand, and sat down right opposite him.

8

KANYE SAT AT THE desk in the corner of his motel room, an open bible before him. He leafed through it, studying the verses that seemed to give to him a divine confirmation of the horrible thing he already knew had happened to his once beloved church. Everywhere he turned, there was confirmation. Peter warned about it: For the time is come that judgment must begin at the house of God: 1 Peter 4:17

Paul warned about it "Let no man deceive you by any means: for that day shall not come, except there come a falling away first, and the man of sin be revealed, the son of perdition; who opposeth and exalteth himself above all that   is called God, or that is worshipped; so that he as God sitteth in the temple of God, shewing himself that he is God." Thessalonians 2:3-4

And Matthew warned about it: When ye therefore shall see the abomination of desolation, spoken of by Daniel the prophet, stand in the holy place (whoso readeth, let him understand:) Then let them which be in Judea flee into the mountains: Matthew 24:15-16

He closed the bible, stood up, and trudged over to the bed. He flopped down, resting his head against the headboard, his mind filled with an awful realization. It was all true. The son of perdition was sitting in the temple of God. The abomination of desolation was standing in the holy place. The church that he once loved had been overrun. And its vicar, Christ, had been replaced by Satan. And that is who he, and the entire Christian church, Catholic, Eastern Orthodox, Anglican, and Protestant, was serving. So much so that they would try to kill a man whose mission was to save humanity from themselves. And they would kill him because a free humanity threatened their own existence.

Kanye took his cell phone off the night stand and looked up his contacts. Near the top of the list was Cardinal Byron Banks. Banks, nearing eighty, was one of Kanye's oldest and dearest friends, and a trusted advisor. Banks knew about Kanye's mission; he was one of the men on the committee that had appointed him to the awful task. And yet, in the twenty-two years since the birth of Adam Landers, he had never discussed this mission with him. Perhaps he simply not wanted to believe that the Cardinal, a man of unceasing kindness, who had given his life in service to the poor, could really be in on this nefarious plot, could really have given himself over to serve Satan.

But of course, it wasn't really that simple. It was not a line that had been crossed boldly, or with careful deliberation. No, it happened gradually, in stages, like a company being bought out by another, bit by bit, piece by piece, until one day the annexing corporation owned a majority of shares and had the deciding vote on matters of corporate policy. This is how the takeover had happened, and good men, like the Cardinal, did not so much make it happen as they failed to actively oppose it. But happen it did. The majority of shares had been acquired by the enemy. And it was something Kanye could not ignore. He called Cardinal Banks, who answered on the third ring. After a brief round of small talk, Kanye, his heart beating fast, got to the reason for his call.

"Cardinal," he said, "I am in a motel in Silverton, Illinois. The man is in my crosshairs. And I am going to kill him. And not in the service of God. How can this be?"

There was silence on the other end for some time. Then Banks said "Kanye, when I first started off as a priest I worked as a missionary in Africa. We were there to bring them the gospel, but also to bring them food and medicine. I wanted so desperately to help those people. But day after day I saw them dying by the dozens. Little children, who had never harmed anyone, baking in the sun, their bellies distended with hunger, their heads swollen, their limbs like sticks, starving to death in the streets like dogs. I began to realize that if this life were a battle between good and evil, then evil was winning. Darkness was swallowing the light; the devil was stronger than God. But the more I read my bible the more I realized that maybe it wasn't so simple. Isaiah 45:7 says: 'I form the light and create darkness. I bring prosperity and create disaster; I the Lord do all these things.'

It's all of God, Kanye. It is not our job to conquer evil in this life, or even to discern its precise source or meaning. That is beyond our powers. Our job is to help people. To salve their wounds, to bring them food, to visit them in prison, to comfort them in their afflictions, to assure them their love ones are in heaven, and that their efforts do not go unrewarded. Our job is to give them the answers they seek, to simplify things for them, so their minds can process them. And this man, Adam, and his mission, will bring only confusion."

"You talk about mankind as if they are a collection of infants," Kanye said. "They *are* infants," the Cardinal replied, "And the church is the world's biggest nursemaid. Who else but infants would believe that you receive forgiveness by confessing your sins to a priest in a dark booth? Or that you receive strength by eating a cookie that's been transformed into the body of Christ? Or that you receive grace by praying the Hail Mary twenty times on a bead of rosaries? Or that you get your dead relatives into heaven quicker by saying novenas for them, or praying to so-called saints on their behalf? They *are* infants, Kanye; they are infants, and our job is to take care of them."

Kanye was shocked to hear the Cardinal talk this way. He had not known that he had grown so cynical. "The church you just described sounds a lot like Satan to me," Kanye said.

"I haven't believed a goddamned thing the church has said for forty years," the cardinal said. "I don't serve the church. I don't serve the devil. I serve man. God doesn't need me; He doesn't need my praise, my songs, my worship, my flattery. He's quite comfortable in His heaven without a word from me. But people do need me, Kanye. Those children if Africa; they needed me. The people dying alone in hospitals; they need me. The people forgotten in prisons; they need me. And it is for them, and them alone, that I wear this clown costume, and do the things I do."

"So, where does that leave me? And my mission? If it's all the same— God and Satan—then why are we serving either one? Why not just follow our own consciences? Because mine tells me that killing is wrong."

"Then you should follow it," the cardinal said. "Maybe if Abraham had said 'No way' when God told him to kill Isaac five thousand years ago, we'd all be better off today."

"Maybe so," Kanye said. And with that, he thanked the old cardinal for his time, and hung up. He didn't know if anything had been resolved or not, but he did no one thing for sure: he had some serious thinking to do.

9

JACK JUST STARED AT her, unable to speak. She looked just like she did in his dreams. Of course, she did. Why wouldn't she? It was the same person. She had her hair pulled back in a bun, and wore no make-up; beauty, in a place like this, was something you did not want to accentuate. Her features were small, her mouth slightly crooked, and her eyes were big brown limpid pools. He felt enveloped by them. She had a kind of latent grin on her lips, like she was trying to hold back a laugh. She was wearing jeans and a loose fitting grey T shirt.

"So, how do you like it so far?" she asked, taking a small bite out of large potato chip. If she recognized him at all, knew anything of him or of their mission, her voice did not betray that knowledge. It was calm and casual, with no hint of excitement or tension. "It's not so bad," he said, his voice not nearly as shaky as he felt. "I've had worse."

And that was the truth; he had. The last two years had been a succession of crappy jobs, one worse than the next.

"Where did you work before?" she asked. "A place in Akron," he replied, trying not to stare too deeply into those all-consuming eyes. "Kind of like this one, actually. A packing plant."

She poured the chips onto the table and said, "Have some."

"Thank you," he said, popping a chip into his mouth, and hoping he remembered how to chew. "So, how long were you there?" she asked. "About three months," Jack replied.

"What about before that?" she asked.

Jack was starting to feel like he was under interrogation, with those eyes serving as heat lamps. "Two months at a vending company in Cedar Lake, Indiana" he said. "And before that, I did a stint in Ashford, Alabama."

"Akron, Cedar Lake, Ashford," Diane said, furrowing her brow. "Are you a drifter?" Jack just shrugged, and said "Yeah, I guess I am."

"What about family?" she asked. "Do you have any?"

"I left home two years ago," Jack said. "That's when the drifting began."

"Must get lonely," she said, her voice still cold and impersonal, in stark contradistinction to her eyes, which bore holes in their target. "Yeah, it does," Jack said. "But I was lonely with my family, too."

"How so?"

"Well, my father was a Pentecostal preacher. Always trying to shove the bible down my throat. He thought . . ." Jack stopped. He could not tell her the real reason for the rift that had developed between himself and his father. That's because it involved the mission, and he wasn't prepared to mention that just yet. So, he just said "Well, you know how it is with parents sometimes."

"Sure," she shrugged, although it was obvious she sensed that he was holding something back.

An awkward silence ensued. It was awkward for him, anyway. He did not think she felt awkward in the least. To fill the silence, he asked "What about you?"

"What about me?" she asked.

"How long have you worked here?"

"About six months," she said, "But something tells me I'll be moving on soon."

"You're not a drifter like me, are you?" he asked.

She smiled slightly—a crooked, wry, beautiful smile—and said "Actually, I am. Except I've been drifting for more than two years. I've been drifting all my life."

"How come?" he asked. He was surprised, yet kind of thrilled, that the conversation had become so personal so fast. Did she talk to everyone this way or did she *know* him? Recognize him? "I never had a family," she said, "I bounced around in foster homes all my life. Then, when I was sixteen I ran away. Been on my own since then."

"And still bouncing around?" Jack added.

"Yeah," she said.

"Guess we're just a couple of strays," Jack noted.

"I guess so," she replied. Another silence ensued, but this one was not so awkward. He was beginning to relax. She had a calm about her that was rubbing off on him.

"So, where are you staying?" she asked.

"Well, until I get enough money for a room, I'm sleeping on a park bench," he said, hoping he didn't sound like he was looking for sympathy; he wasn't. "Well, we can't have that," she said. "You'll just have to stay with me for a while."

Jack's heart almost stopped. Was he hearing her right? Did she just invite him to *live* with her? The thought so overwhelmed him that for a moment he actually considered declining the offer. But then he came to his senses, and said "Really? You would do that for me, a perfect stranger?" She just shrugged and said, "Us strays have to stick together."

He looked at her with awe, and suddenly the love he already felt for her magnified itself a thousand-fold. The feeling was so intense that for a moment he thought he might dissolve into tears. Instead he took a deep breath and said "I guess so. Thank you."

"No sweat," she said. "There's just one thing I need to know first."

"Sure."

"What's your name?"

Jack smiled, embarrassed. "Jack," he said. "Jack Horn. What's yours."

"Diane Foster."

Diane Foster, Jack thought. He knew that wasn't her real name any more than his real name was Jack. Her real name was Eve. He wondered if *she* knew that. "Now I have to ask *you* something," Jack said.

"Shoot."

"How do you feel about cats?"

"You got a cat? You don't even have a home."

"It sort of adopted me. We sleep together on the park bench."

She crinkled her nose and said "Sure, bring it along."

⌣

The rest of the day flew by fast. Faster than any day Jack could remember. All day he had that light-as-a-feather feeling he had gotten the first time he had seen her. Only there were concerns, too. In the space of a day this girl had gone from a glorious phantom in his dreams to someone he worked with to someone he was going to *live* with. Exactly how was he supposed to pull this off? How could he act normally around her? How much should he tell her about what he knew? And how soon? And what did she know, if anything? What if he told her, and she thought he was crazy, and never wanted to see him again? He didn't know the answers to any of those questions. He decided to simply take it slow, letting things play out one day at a time. For the first few days, he would say nothing.

When quitting time rolled around, he punched out and waited for Diane down in the lobby. He did not have to wait long. She got off the elevator, along with three others, and they made their way into the parking lot, to her car. She pulled out, made a quick left onto Old Hook, then a quick right onto Main, which she took to the park, where they got out together and made their way to the picnic area.

"Here kitty kitty kitty," Jack cooed, snapping his fingers, and looking around for signs of feline life. Nothing. Jack and Diane exchanged a kind of puzzled stare, then Jack started in again with the here kittys. This time Diane joined in. Within moments the cat appeared, looking cautiously at the new party, then walking briskly over to Jack and rubbing up against his leg. Jack scooped it up in his arms, nuzzling its head with his chin, and brought it back to the car.

Diane retraced her path, back to Old Hook, and took it all the way to the end. Then she made a few more rights and lefts, each one taking them deeper into the outskirts of town, where there were less homes and more trees, trailers, and dirt roads, until they arrived at her place—a basement apartment beneath a large colonial that was only one of a few homes on a mostly deserted street.

Diane parked right in front of the house. Jack followed her out, down a flight of stairs that ran along the side of the house, to her door. She unlocked the door, and held it open for her new guests. Jack wanted to say "Nice place you've got here" just to be polite, but it would have been too big of a lie, and Diane would have surely called him on it. Instead he just went "Hmmm . . . interesting," to which Diane replied "Yeah, I know . . . it's a wreck."

"But a very cozy one," Jack said, putting down the cat and taking a stroll around. "Come one, I'll give you the grand tour," she said, pointing out the highlights and lowlights of her humble basement abode. On one wall was a black couch with badly beaten cushions, and an equally beaten up accent chair beside it. Opposite the couch was a TV on an entertainment center. Just past the couch was a table with two chairs, and past that, a kitchen with no room for a table. Opposite the table in the living room was a hallway, leading to a bedroom on one side and another bedroom and a bathroom on the other. All of the rooms were very small.

"I hope your landlord won't mind my being here," Jack said, "not to mention my furry friend." He pointed at the cat, who was on top of the couch, stretching itself. "I don't think she'll mind," Diane said. "The owner is very old, barely even aware of what's going on. I think she should probably be in a nursing home by now."

"I see," Jack said. "That's too bad."

"Yeah, well . . . It is what it is." She paused for a few moments, staring at him with those big eyes, then said, "Well, you can get settled in now if you want. I'm going to take a shower. I'll bring you some sheets for the bed later on. And after that . . . I'm going to cook us a big dinner."

"That sounds great," he said, taken aback by her hospitality. With that, she turned and went off to her bedroom. He did the same. He tossed his back pack on the bed and unpacked. It was going to feel great eating real food tonight, not to mention sleeping in a real bed. The fact that he would be doing it with *her* . . . well, that just made it a million times better.

He settled in quickly; there wasn't much to unpack—just a few toiletries and some cloths. And of course, his glock, which he put in a dresser under some pants.

And that was that. He had a new home.

He heard the shower running in the next room. He waited for it to stop, waited for her to finish up, and then he took his turn. After showering and getting dressed, he went back into the living room. Diane was already in the kitchen working on dinner. "Is there anything I can do to help?" he asked, feeling guilty about being the beneficiary of so much hospitality. "No, I'm good," she said. "Besides, there's only room for one person at a time in here."

"I get it," Jack said, plopping himself on the couch as the cat curled up in his lap. He stroked it behind the ears. It purred deeply. "So, what about a name for this cat?" he called out. "Oh, I don't know," she said, "Is it a male or a female?"

"Male."

"I had a cat named Tabby as a kid. How about that?"

"I don't think she looks like a Tabby," Jack said.

"Probably not," Diane agreed.

"What are some good cat names?"

"I don't know. Mittens. Buttons. Fluffy."

"Maybe we should work on it later," Jack said.

"I can't cook and think at the same time," Diane explained.

"I understand. I can't cook at all."

"As long as you can eat, that's enough for tonight."

"I can," Jack said, falling deeper in love with her with every word she spoke.

∽

"Dinner's served," Diane announced a short time later, placing a large platter of roasted chicken on the table. Sharing the platter with the chicken was a large serving of carrots, rice, and red potatoes. "God, that looks good," Jack observed, his mouth watering. "I hope it tastes good," Diane replied. "I wouldn't worry about that," Jack said, picking up the carving knife, and slicing the chicken into thin pieces, placing some on her plate, and some on his own. He took a mouthful. "It's delicious," he said. "Where'd you learn to cook like this?"

"When you grow up in foster homes," she answered, "you learn to do a lot of things."

"I see," Jack said. He could sense the hurt in those words. *A lot* of hurt. The cat sidled up to him, looking up, hoping to share in the feast. He dangled a thin piece of meat over its head and let it nibble away. "Have you thought of a name for him yet?" Diane asked. "Not yet," Jack said, furrowing his brow in thought. "How about . . . Eve?"

Diane looked down at her lap, saying nothing. It was the first time since he met her that she displayed any trace of discomfort. The two sat in awkward silence for several moments. Then she looked up, fixed her eyes on him, and said "I know about our mission."

Jack just looked at her disbelievingly, his fork frozen midway between his plate and his mouth. "Yeah," she repeated, "I know about the mission."

"I can't tell you how relieved I am to hear that," Jack said.

"I can imagine," Diane replied, "Wouldn't be much fun saving the world alone, right?"

"Is that what we're supposed to be doing?" Jack asked. "Saving the world?"

"Well, what else could it be?" she asked. "Leading mankind to the Garden of Eden. Isn't that the same as saving the world?"

"I don't know, maybe the whole thing is just a wild goose chase," Jack said.

"That's a *terrible* thing to say," she snarled, and suddenly those two big brown orbs locked on him in a harsh, withering glare; he felt, quite literally, like a deer in the headlights. "I'm just saying," he replied, floundering for words "that we really don't *know* anything yet. I can't speak for you, but the messages *I've* gotten are long on drama and short on detail. What about you?"

"Well," she said, gritting her teeth "I haven't received any *specific* instructions yet, but . . .'"

"But what?" Jack pressed.

"But that doesn't mean they're not forthcoming!" she said, her voice rising about two octaves, to just a hair beneath a shout. Jack was taken aback; he did not take her for the emotional type. "Well, to be honest," Jack said, suspecting he was on the wrong course, but plodding ahead anyway: "I'm not sure I even *want* any instructions!"

"What do you mean?" she asked accusingly. "I mean," Jack said, a note of annoyance creeping into his own voice, "this mission has ruined my life. I never asked for any of this, and I don't even want it."

"Well, I never asked for it either, but it is what it is. I mean . . . we were divinely appointed to provide a great service to mankind. Doesn't that mean anything to you?"

Jack did not know how to answer. In truth, he had never actually looked at it that way. He had only considered how it affected *him*; he had never thought about how it might affect others. "I guess I never thought about it that way," Jack said sheepishly. "Well, you should," Diane said, her tone of angry indignation replaced by one of gentle admonishment. "The burden to yourself won't seem as bad if you think about others. I mean, just look at Christ as an example."

Oh God, no, Jack thought. Please don't let her be a born again evangelical nut job. "You're not . . . *religious*?" he asked, pronouncing the word as if it represented the worse disease one could imagine.

Sighing, Diane said "No, I'm not *religious*, but I have prepared myself for this mission. I have studied the bible extensively, along with Greek and Hebrew, and anything else that I thought might be of relevance to this task."

Jack was dumbfounded. Here he had spent his whole life resenting his calling while she had spent hers *preparing* for it. He was more interested in *her* than in their mission; for her it was just the opposite. He wondered if she had any interest in him at all. "Well, he said," trying to make light of it, "at least one of us is ready for what's to come."

She just gave him a sneer and said, "I hope so." For a moment they just sat there, frozen, then, as if by mutual decision, they resumed their dinner without speaking about their mission again for the rest of the evening.

10

THE TWELVE MEN, ELEVEN Cardinals and the Pope, all clothed in their vestments, descended the long staircase that lead to the basement chamber of the apostolic palace in Vatican City, Rome. The chamber was a large round room, ringed by massive white columns, with a high ceiling and stone walls with a variety of figures carved into them. The figures were of ancient gods, beasts, angels, demons and an assortment of other strange and exotic creatures. The only light came from lanterns, which sat in holders that had been anchored into the walls. The room was dark and dank, filled with shadows and an eerie silence.

The men spread out into a large circle in the center of the room. Hanging from the ceiling in the middle of the circle was a rope. The men knit their hands together in a prayerful pose and bowed their heads. Then they began to chant in Latin. *Tuum est regnum, tuum regnum venero ut.* The Kingdom is yours; come take your kingdom.

The chant continued for five minutes. Then the pope stood in the middle of the circle, stretched his arms out wide and said in a booming voice: "When ye therefore shall see the abomination of desolation, spoken of by Daniel the prophet, stand in the holy place, Then let them which be in Judea flee into the mountains . . ."

And the cardinals declared in response: *Ipse stat in locum sanctum* He stands in the Holy Place!

The pope continued: "Let no man deceive you by any means: for that day shall not come, except there come a falling away first, and the man of sin be revealed, the son of perdition; who opposeth and exalteth himself above all that is called God, or that is worshipped; so that he as God sitteth in the temple of God, shewing himself that he is God.

The cardinals declared in response: *Venit sedens in templo!* Come sit in the temple!

Then the pope pulled on the rope. A whole opened up in the ceiling and a huge cross dropped down, stopping just inches from the floor. It was inverted, with the figure of Christ attached. One by one the Cardinals approached it and pissed on it, declaring *Ut benedicat tibi*—I renounce you—as they did so.

Then they gathered back in a circle and took up a new chant: *tuun est Ecclesia nostra; tolle tibi sedem in templo.* Our church is yours; take your seat in the temple.

Over and over again they made the dreadful pronouncement, each time their voices growing louder, until they were shouting it out at the top of their lungs, their bodies trembling, their voices straining, their brows slick with sweat. Amidst their shouts the first plumes of smoke began to arise from the floor below them. Slowly it grew denser and blacker. The acrid stench of hell fire filled the air as the figures in the stone walls began to pulse with life, growling and screeching in glorious celebration.

When it was over, they pulled the cross back up into the ceiling, wiped the smoke residue off their vestments, and made their way back up the stairs, where they would continue business as usual.

11

JACK LAY THERE ON his bed, head propped against the headboard, thinking about the day's events. Mostly he was thinking about his conversation with Diane, which had ended with a kind of silent, mutual agreement not to discuss the matter any further that evening. The rest of the evening's conversation pertained entirely to mundane matters of mutual interest, like the dinner they ate together, the job they shared, and the movie they watched on the sofa before retiring to their respective bedrooms. Some more consideration was given to the matter of naming their cat, and they finally decided to call it Smokey.

He rolled over to his side and stared at the watch on his dresser. It was twelve P.M.. He had already been lying there for an hour, thinking. They covered a lot of ground at dinner, but there were so many things they didn't cover. So many questions he still had. Were they still trying to kill her too? And if so, why? Why were the two of them regarded as threats, and to whom? And what about their mission? What was it exactly? When was it to begin? And what about *them*? Did she dream about him the way he dreamt about her? Did she have feelings for him? Those were just a few of the questions he had; there were many more, and right now, they were playing and re-playing in his mind like a record with the needle stuck, blocking him from sleeping.

To make matters worse, he did not even have the cat to curl up with; the darned thing had taken a decided preference for Diane and had chosen to spend the night with her. Of course, cats never were never known for their loyalty; that was more of a dog thing. But at least he did have a bed tonight. That was a substantial improvement over a park bench. And while the cover of the night sky might have a certain charm, it was no substitute for an actual brick and mortar ceiling. In point of fact he had it pretty good right now, if he could just quell the crush of questions that were crowding his brain. If only he had a fraction of Diane's faith. Or her commitment. But he didn't, and he doubted that he ever would. But then again, he had never really expected to see Diane in the flesh, and here he was, so what did he know?

The questions continued to swirl in his brain, but gradually, they slowed down, until finally his eyes grew heavy and slumber overtook him.

Moments later he was dreaming.

He was in a garden, alone, surrounded only by the sights and sounds of nature. In the distance a woman was walking toward him. Like him, she was naked. She walked slowly, with great deliberation. Her arms were slightly outstretched, palms facing up. Her hips swayed with each long, graceful stride. As she got closer, a small, wry smile crept onto her lips. She stopped just feet before him, drinking him in with her big, brown eyes, then brought her hands up slowly to his cheeks, tickling his skin with the tips of her soft, tapered fingers. Her touch was like an electrical current, sending waves of pleasure through his body. She began to draw his face toward her waiting lips. As she did, she slid one hand behind him, down his back, and began moving it in circles. The warmth from her hands was like nothing he had ever felt before. By the time their lips touched, his legs were like jello; he realized he was not even standing up on his own power; she was holding him up. As their lips touched he felt himself on the precipice of an ecstasy beyond anything he had ever imagined; he needed only to move a little further, a little *deeper* into her. But just as that was about to happen she drew back, like she always did at this point. Then she moved her head back and forth in a gesture that said *no*. And when he reached for her, she was gone.

12

CLAD IN A T-SHIRT and a pair of short sweat pants, Kanye sat at the foot of the bed, remote in hand, trying to find something to watch before turning in for the night. This would be his last night at the motel. His last night at *any* motel, chasing Jack Horn around, tracking his movements, planning to kill him. He had made up his mind. He was leaving tomorrow morning. Leaving the town of Silverton, leaving this mission, and leaving the church he had served for twenty years. He would have left tonight, but he had a slight headache and he preferred driving during the day.

There was a knock at the door—a soft, almost apologetic tapping, as if the person really didn't want to bother him. That was good; he didn't want to be bothered. He walked over to the door and opened it. Standing before him was a beautiful young woman in a sliver robe, cinched at the waist, holding a bottle of wine. She had a purse slung around her shoulder. She was black, like him, with a gorgeous mane of white hair that flowed gently down her shoulders and neck. She had sparkling turquoise eyes, full lips, and skin like glass. On her feet were diamond encrusted slippers that matched the color of her robe, and in her hair, a few inches above her left ear, a solitary short stemmed flower.

For a moment Kanye could not breath; he just stood there, mouth agape, staring at this heavenly vision. She smiled at him, revealing pearly white teeth that glistened marvelously against the backdrop of her black skin. "Got a little something for you," she said, holding up the bottle of wine. "I heard it was your favorite." It was a red Merlot. It *was* his favorite. "Yes," he said in a shaky voice, "It is. How did you know?"

"Oh, I know things," she said, running a finger down his arm as she stepped into the room. She strolled over to the bed and placed her purse on the night stand. Then she got into the bed, resting her back against the headboard, and patted the mattress, saying, "Well, aren't you gonna join me?"

Kanye did not know how to respond. For thirty years, he had kept his vows of celibacy. And now, on the eve of his intended departure from the church, comes this temptation. As if reading his mind, the woman said, "One drink isn't going to hurt, is it?"

"Well . . . I suppose not," Kanye said, approaching the bed. He got on it next to her. "That's better," the woman said, smiling, then retrieved two wine glasses and a cork screw from her purse. "Would you like to do the honors?" she asked, handing him the bottle and the cork screw. He took them from her, his hands quivering slightly. He steadied himself and dug the cork screw into the cork, wrestled with it for a bit, then popped it. A little spilled onto the mattress.

She took the bottle from him and poured some into one glass, which she handed to him, and some into another, which she kept for herself. She held her glass up and said, "To pleasure" and took a big sip. He did the same. Then she opened up her robe a little, revealing the inner outline of her breasts. She took another sip and moved closer to him. "Do you like it?" she asked, smiling coyly. He didn't know if she meant the wine or her, although he suspected that she had both things in mind. "Yes," he said weakly, feeling very much like a teenager during his first sexual tryst. "Good," she said, sliding her free hand behind his head and pulling it toward her lips. Just inches before they touched she whispered, "I want you to enjoy yourself."

As he sat there frozen by a mixture of indecision and pleasure, she took his glass in her fingertips and placed it on the nightstand, along with her own. Then she pulled her robe off. She was naked underneath. Her breasts were like two perfectly round melons and her legs long and shapely. Looking at him and smiling, she licked two fingers and slid them slowly down her torso, beginning at her breasts, moving to her navel, and finally between her legs, where she began slowly rubbing, as a series of soft, sensual murmurs of pleasure escaped her full, moist lips. The whole time she kept her eyes locked on Kanye's—a kind of warm, invisible embrace that he could feel almost as intensely as an actual physical touch.

"Well," she asked, "Aren't you going to join me?" Quivering, he undressed and fell into her arms. Her embrace was like nothing he had ever experienced, or even imagined, before. Her lips, pressed against his, sent ripples of ecstasy shooting through him. Her breath, so soft against his skin, tickling his ears, making him shiver from head to toe. And her voice, when she did speak, was like the gentle strumming of a violin, lulling him into a dreamlike state of almost unbearable peace. For several hours, she took him to new and unimaginable heights of bliss, each one more incredible than the last.

When it was over, she lay there beside him on the bed, her head propped up against his chest, and said "*The pleasure you feel now; you can have it every day; would you like that?*"

He nodded helplessly. "Good," she said, "then all you have to do is stay here and kill the boy. Do you think you can do that for me?" His exhilaration quickly turned to dread. He did want this woman, wanted her more than anything, but not at such a cost. "I can't do that," he said.

"Oh, come on, now," she said, running a finger through the hairs on his chest, "I'm sure you could." Her finger was hot, like a coal. Plumes of smoke rose up from his chest as she pressed harder. "In fact," she said, "I'm sure you *will*."

The pain was intense. He tried to move but couldn't. "Please . . . let me go," he pleaded in a barely audible voice.

"First, you have to promise," she said, placing her palm flat against his chest. It felt like an iron was searing his flesh. Smoke wafted up in thick plumes now, and he could smell his flesh burning. "Promise or you will feel this way all the time," she said. He cried out in agony, but still he resisted giving his assent to her awful demand. She began moving her hand in circles, searing him deeper and deeper, until the pain became unbearable, and he cried out "Okay, okay; I will do it!"

"Good boy," she said, and removed her hand from his chest. The smoke subsided and, except for a slight residual burning sensation, he felt nothing. The woman put her robe back on and headed for the door. "Enjoy the wine," she said, blowing him a kiss as she left the motel room.

13

FOR THE SECOND STRAIGHT night, Diane made dinner for them. This time she kept it simple: steak and fries. And this time Jack was smart enough not to mix business with food; he made no mention of their mission. When dinner was finished Jack cleared off the table, did the dishes, and took out the trash. He lingered outside by the curb, thinking. What exactly should he do when he went back inside? He hardly knew this girl, and yet he was *living* with her. He had met her just two days ago, and yet he loved her. As he went back inside he knew only this: they had to talk. Yesterday was a start, but then they backed off. Tonight, they had to do some serious talking, no matter how uncomfortable it might get.

Fortunately for him, when he went back inside, it seemed like Diane had pretty much the same idea. The TV was still not on, and she seemed to be just kind of waiting for him. He sat down across from her on the accent chair. "So," he said with a deep breath "Why don't we get to know each other a little better?" To his relief, Diane said "Yeah, I think that would be a great place to start."

And then she proceeded to fill him in on some facts. Like him, news of her mission came by way of periodic voices in her head and visions. Unlike him, the dreams she had of the two of them together were not of a romantic nature. He also learned that wherever she went, she was tracked. She had survived two attempts on her life; during the second her then step-father was killed protecting her as she climbed down a fire escape. She related these facts in a clinical fashion, the way you might explain your job history to a prospective employer. It became clear to him that she regarded their relationship, at this point in time, essentially as a business arrangement, and had no immediate plans to move it past that point.

It was his turn. Like Diane, he related as much information as he could, including some details about the rift that the mission had caused between himself and his father. For his father—a Pentecostal preacher—Jack's divine appointment was a point of pride, and a validation of his own piety. The fact that it kept them on the run like criminals didn't seem to bother him. Jack had come to blame his father for being given the unwelcome task in the first place.

Jack also told her about the dreams, although he did not mention their highly sexual content. He told her only that he had dreamt about her.

As for the mission, they were equally clueless. Neither knew what it entailed or when it would begin. Both, however, believed that now that they had found it other, it was about to commence. Maybe, in some way, it already had.

After clearing the air, Jack felt a sense of relief. He could see that she felt it too. They watched an old movie together, with Smokey alternating between her lap and his, and talked normally, about normal things, for the film's duration. At the film's conclusion they said their good nights and made their separate ways to their respective bedrooms. Smokey, of course, went with her.

Jack didn't dream that night. He did, however, wake with a start in the middle of the night, feeling groggy and nervous and beset by a suffocating sense of imminent danger. Something wasn't right. He picked up his watch on the nightstand and pressed the little light button on the side; it read three A.M. Jack was usually a sound sleeper. He didn't wake unless something woke him. What was waking him at three A.M.? Or maybe a better question was . . . Who? As quietly as possible, he crept over to the dresser, slid it open, and removed his glock. As he did, he could hear the movement. Footsteps. Someone was out there, and he knew it wasn't Diane, and it damn sure wasn't Smokey. It was the sound of a stranger, lurking around in the living room, probably clad in black, with a stocking on his face, intending to either rob them, kill them, or both.

Jack was not going to wait around for that to happen. Gun raised, he threw his door open and burst out into the living room to the sight of a man fleeing through the front door. Jack followed but slammed his bare toe against the leg of the entertainment center. He howled in pain, dancing around on one foot for several seconds, before getting his bearings back. By that time Diane was out there with him, cinching a robe around her waist, as Smokey moved about underfoot. "Someone broke in," was all Jack had time to say as he dashed out the front door in pursuit of the intruder. But when he looked around he saw nothing. He had gotten away.

Jack went back inside. "He's gone," he growled angrily. He would have loved nothing more than to put a bullet hole through the SOB that had been hunting him like a crocodile all these years. "Guess we know how he got in," Diane said, pointing at the living room window. A big section of glass had been cut out, probably with a laser guided precision tool, and lay there on the rug. "Lovely," Jack said simply. They had been found. Jack knew what that meant. It meant what it always meant. Time to move on. Whoever that man was, he was part of a larger operation. And that operation, whatever it was, now knew of his precise location. That meant if he—if they—didn't move on quickly they would be dead. It was that simple.

"So," Diane said, staring at the large, circular hole in the window, "when do we leave?" Jack thought about it for a moment. They could wait until morning, of course. But if they did it might be too late. He shrugged. "How's right now sound?"

"Sounds good to me," Diane said. On that note the two went off to their respective bedrooms and packed their things. Diane left a note for her landlord on the living room table, along with some rent money in an envelope, and within minutes they were in the car and on the road.

41

14

KANYE WAS STILL SWEATING when he pulled into the driveway of the Red Roof Inn and got out of the car. He had almost gotten them, but the kid was too smart, too fast, too alert. Or maybe he was just too damned noisy, too clumsy, or too stupid. Or maybe, just maybe, a part of him didn't want to succeed in this nefarious mission. Maybe he just wasn't ready to kill an innocent man, no matter how many visits he received from demonic forces who had other ideas. Whatever the reason, he had failed. That was all that mattered; it was all his superiors would want to know.

Briefcase in hand, he got out of the car, walked over to his motel room door, and went inside. He put the briefcase, which contained his gun and glass cutter, in the closet, then sat down at the desk in the corner of the room. He slipped a hand in his pocket, pulled out his cell phone, and dialed the number for Cardinal Salvatore Ricci. Ricci was his immediate supervisor, a Cardinal for over thirty years, and the Pope's right-hand man. He would not be happy about the report he was about to receive. But then again, Kanye was not very happy either. He did not appreciate being conscripted for duty under threat of being burned alive.

The cardinal answered on the fourth ring, his voice drowsy. It was four A.M. Getting right to the point, Kanye said simply "It's Kanye. I failed."

"Give me the details," the Cardinal said simply, his voice calm and business like. "I made the attempt at 3:00 A.M.," Kanye said, "The boy was staying at the apartment of a girl who, if I'm not mistaken, is the one who will be accompanying him on the mission."

"You mean Eve," the cardinal said.

"Yes. I broke into their apartment, but the boy was ready for me with a gun in hand. I was forced to flee."

"Okay," the cardinal said. "Listen to me. We anticipated this possibility. We have assembled a team of trained assassins, all with military background and weapons training. They will be assisting you. We will get this done; it just might take a little more time than we had hoped. We were foolish to think it would be so easy. We are expanding the operation; operatives all over the country will be searching for them. For now, you just get back on their trail and keep in touch. We will get this thing done."

"Yes sir," Kanye said simply. He had no desire to extend the conversation beyond what was necessary. He hung up. Then he got up, kicked of his shoes, and flopped down onto the bed. The mission could wait. He needed a nap.

PART 2

THE SEVEN CITIES

15

So long Silverton, Jack thought as the town faded, both literally and figuratively, in the rear-view mirror of Diane's 2002 blue Dodge. Jack watched with silent admiration as she drove along in the pre-dawn darkness. She was as cool as ice. You would never guess to look at her face that she had just been forced to flee her home in the middle of the night. She had the grim expression of one who had accepted her fate.

After snaking her way down some side streets, she got on interstate 10 and headed West. Jack checked on Smokey, who was already fast asleep in the back seat. All they had taken with them were two backpacks—hers and his. Like him, she had learned to travel light.

After about ten minutes, she got onto route 55, still heading West. They drove for an hour without saying a word. Diane broke the silence as they passed a sign for Roy Rogers, which was up at the next rest stop. "I'm hungry," she said, "How about you?"

"Starving," Jack said.

"Good," Diane replied, and pulled into the nearly empty rest stop.

"What about ol' Smokey?" Jack asked. Diane turned around, looking at the cat. It was sprawled out on its side, sleeping peacefully, it's legs fully extended on the seat. "He'll be fine," Diane said. "Yeah, I guess so," Jack agreed.

They got out and made their way into the restaurant, stopping at the counter to study the menu overhead. They were the only ones on line, and there was only one other person in the restaurant—a scraggly old man, seated alone in a corner, sipping a cup of coffee. Diane ordered a number four, which consisted of two pieces of chicken, two sides, and a soda. Jack did the same. They waited for their orders, then took them over to a table by the window.

Neither said much beyond ordinary small talk as they ate. Jack knew why. They both sensed the gravity of the situation. Having to flee for their safety was nothing new for either of them. But this time was different. Now that they were together, they both sensed that their mission was about to begin, if it hadn't already. And yet they both remained in the dark as to what that mission actually was, and as to what they were supposed to do. They were like two soldiers, sitting on a rock in a swamp somewhere, waiting for orders. Jack did not like the feeling, and he could tell she didn't either. Breaking the silence, Jack asked "So, where do you want to go?"

Diane thought about it for several moments, then said "I want to go to Disneyland."

"Seriously?" Jack asked.

"Why not?" Diane replied, shrugging. And she had a point. Did it really matter where they went at this point? They might just as well go someplace cool. "Sounds good to me," Jack said, staring into Diane's big, brown eyes. As he did, he felt a sudden urge to tell her how he felt. To tell her about the dreams, about his love for her, about how he had loved her for the last ten years, about how she was the only bright spot in the otherwise dreary landscape of his life right now. Why not? Why not tell her? What did have to lose? But there was something in her face—a distance, a *desire* for distance—that told him it would not be a good idea. As caring and decent a person as she was, she was also cold and clinical—perhaps, Jack suspected, even pathologically so. And he knew it had something to do with her foster home upbringing. She had been hurt, probably many times. And each time comprised another brick in the wall she had built around herself. Jack wondered if he would ever be able to scale that wall.

They finished their meals, piled all the garbage on their trays, and dumped them in the receptacles. Then they used the restrooms and made their way back to the car. Smokey was still fast asleep. Diane started up the car and pulled out, back onto route 55. "So," Jack said, "Do you know how to get to Disneyland?"

"Well," Diane said, "As long as we're going West, we're going in the right direction. But if we need it, there's a map in the glove compartment."

"Works for me," Jack said.

After another hour on the road the sun started to come up, and Diane shut off the headlights. Jack was already starting to forget Silverton. Of course, he had only been there for a few days; there wasn't much to forget. He would not miss Manus Manufacturing; that much he knew. But he knew it wasn't just Silverton he was leaving behind. It was a chapter of his life. That chapter was over. A new one—whatever it was—had begun. And that chapter included something that was good, something that was bad, and something he could not really put in either column just yet. The presence of Diane in his life was most definitely a good thing. Continuing to be hunted like a crocodile was a bad thing. And the beginning of the mission . . . only time would tell.

Diane turned on the radio. The distinctive guitar solo that opened up the song was unmistakable. Although the song was from a different era, Jack had heard it a thousand times, and he loved it. It was John Mellencamp's iconic *Jack and Diane*. When she realized what was playing, Diane threw her head back, broke out into a huge, embarrassed grin, and cried out "Oh, no! God, noooooo!!!!" They looked at each other briefly, cringing, then turned away as the words came flying through the speakers: *Little ditty 'bout Jack and Diane / two American kids growing up in the heartland . . .*

They made light of it, but it did not feel like an accident to Jack. It was not an accident that this song was playing, or that their real names, Adam and Eve, were no less joined in the common parlance than their assumed ones. This song, playing at this moment, was not a coincidence; it was a commemoration, and they both knew it. And about midway through it their eyes met again, and this time there was no laughter. This time their eyes were saying *Okay, we've been brought together; so be it.* As the song wound down, Jack felt an intense, almost painful oneness with Diane, and with it, a terrible longing for her.

About an hour later Diane said, "I have to pee," and they began looking for the next rest stop. "You *know* that women have smaller bladders than men?" she said. "I've heard something to that effect," Jack replied. Moments later she took the exit for the rest stop. The stop, however, was not close, and she had to drive for several minutes and make a number of turns before they were there. Jack hoped they could find their way back onto the highway.

As she parked the car, the cat jerked to life and growled loudly. "I'll feed our furry friend while we wait," Jack said as Diane ran off. Jack popped the trunk open and rummaged through his back pack for food. Luckily, he had brought a few cans of Purina cat chow with him. He popped it open, hopped in the back seat, and held the can while the cat devoured his meal.

By the time he was finished Diane had returned. Jack got back in the front seat as she pulled out and headed back the way she came. At least that was the intent. But it was easier said than done and they soon found themselves going around in the same circle three times. "Okay," Diane said, showing some frustration, "Let's try this one more time." They made a right onto a street called Decatur, drove down a short way, then followed the sign for route 55, which led them around a long, curving bend in the shape of a C, then, rather than emerging on route 55, they found themselves on a street called Chambers Bridge, and then back on Decatur. "Damn it," Diane said. This was the most pissed off Jack had seen her in their short time together.

She pulled over, stopped, and threw her hands up. "Want to give it a shot?" she asked Jack. He shrugged and said "Sure." They switched places. Jack took a moment to look around and get his bearings. All around them, on both sides of the road, was nothing but empty marshland lined with trees. He started driving, slowing down at the route 55 sign, followed the bend, around in a C, and, just like Diane, wound up on Chambers Bridge Road. Like Decatur, the road was lined by marshes and trees on both sides. Off to the left, about half way up, was a spooky looking old house with brown shingles, a sagging roof, and large windows peering out the side, with the shades drawn. It was the only sign of habitation in the circle they had been traveling around in.

Now it was Jack's turn to stop. "Well, this is strange," he said. "Yeah," Diane agreed. "All right," Jack said, "let's change things up a bit this time." He drove down Chambers Bridge and made the right onto Decatur as before. But this time he passed the sign for route 55 and made the next right. "I think this is the way we came last time," he said, "I think that sign for 55 was pointing ahead, to *this* turn off."

"Oh, I see," Diane said, as if a great mystery had been solved, although it was really just a small one; in fact, it was a common error that drivers made all the time. Jack followed the new turn off around the bend. To his great dismay, however, it led them right back to Chambers Bridge Road and the spooky house. "Oh, come on!" Diane hissed. "Well, this is fucked up," Jack noted, and gunned the engine, speeding ahead for another try. "This can't be right. Let me try again." Again, he passed the first sign, took the second, and wound up back on Chambers Bridge. "This is so fucked!" he said.

What he didn't say was that with each rotation they made around the area it seemed to be getting darker and the branches of the trees seemed to be multiplying. "Let's try it the other way again," Jack said, hoping the nervousness he felt was not showing in his voice. He tried the first way again, and again they wound up in the same spot. And this time he was certain that the branches had gotten bigger, reaching out into the road, like gnarled claws trying to grab at them. And it had gotten darker. He was sure of it. Diane, damn her, was so calm that he couldn't tell if she was noticing it too.

When it became more uncomfortable to keep it in than to say something, he said "Are you noticing anything different than when we first started?" She shot him a quick glance, as if he'd said something horrible, then stared back out at the road. "Jesus," she said, "I was hoping it was my imagination." He looked at her, shook his head, and said simply "It wasn't."

"Shit," she said.

"Yeah, you said it," Jack repeated. He had slowed down now, as he turned onto Decatur. If there was any way to make it out of there he wanted to do it now, before it got dark. Darker. It was already kind of dark. Off to the sides, in the marshes, he saw a thin mist of smoke starting to form over the waters.

He kept on driving, turning right at the 55 sign. As he turned, he thought he saw something off to his right move. Not an animal. Not a person. It was . . . a branch. It seemed to stretch out as he passed it. As if reaching for him. He kept driving, hoping against hope, that somehow, someway, he would emerge out of this bend, which had been marked with a sign for route 55, onto route 55.

It didn't happen. Once again, they were on Chambers Bridge road. And now, as he looked up the road, his heart skipped a beat. The entire road was dark and filled with overhanging branches, reaching deep into the road, like hundreds of gnarled old hands trying to swallow up the pavement. As he drove he could feel—and hear—the crunching of wood beneath his wheels. And off to the side, in the marshes, the smoke was thickening. So was the darkness. He had to strain now to see. He looked at Diane, his eyes wide. "What the fuck is going on?" he whispered, his voice quivering. "I have absolutely no idea," she whispered. The cat yelped in the backseat. She reached over and pulled it onto her, scooping it up into her chest, and cradling it, as if for dear life.

He kept driving as the mostly bare branches all around them continued to sprout, as if being nourished from above by some super concentrated, miracle nutrient. He could actually see the growth now, in real time, as he drove along, as if the branches were literally reaching out for them.

Off to their sides, the smoke in the marshes was thickening, rising up in a thick cloud, while the last rays of light faded, shrouding them in a midnight darkness. Jack had to crane his neck and strain his eyes to see where he was going. He was just about to suggest they leave the car and try making a run for it when up ahead he saw a most unexpected sight. It was the figure of man. He was standing on the side of the road—Diane's side—looking their way, with his thumb outstretched. He wore a white trench coat, which is probably the only reason Jack could see him. Jack looked at Diane, who had also seen the man. "What do you think?" he asked, "Should we pick him up?"

"It's not like we've got anything to lose," Diane said. "You could say that again," Jack agreed. He pulled over. Through the window Diane said, "Get in" and the man obeyed, opening the door and sliding into the back seat. They turned around to have a better look at him. He was an older man, about sixty, with a scraggly grey beard, thinning hair, and the reddish eyes and complexion of a man who had imbibed one too many cheap bottles of gin. The man had a friendly expression on his weathered face; if he knew there was something amiss out there, he gave no hint of it. Either he was completely plastered, Jack thought, or just dumb as a stone. "Are you okay?" Diane asked. "Never better," the man answered. "Hey, that's a nice cat," he said, "Mind if I pet it?" He reached out and stroked the cat's hindquarters. Jack and Diane shared an incredulous glance. "Um . . .," Jack said, "I don't know if you noticed, but something really bad is going on out there."

"Oh, I noticed," the man said, nodding his head. "Why do you think I'm here?"

"Pardon me?" Jack said. The man sighed. "I'm surprised you kids haven't figured it out by now, but you guys aren't in Kansas anymore!"

"Come again?" Jack said.

"Well," the man went on, "In the *real* world, the branches of trees don't grow at an exponential rate in order to devour the people around them."

Jack and Diane looked at each other, eyes wide, then back at the man. "You mean we're not in the real world anymore?" Diane asked. The man touched the tip of his nose with his forefinger and cried out "Bingo! You get a prize, young lady." Then the man chuckled and said, "Allow me to introduce myself, guys: my name is Brady and I'm your guide."

"Guide for what?" Jack asked.

"Guide for this," Brady said, pointing out the window. "I'm your guide for the first leg of what will hopefully be your tour through seven cities on your way to leading man back to the Garden of Eden." He paused briefly, allowing them a moment to process his words, then continued "This is the first city. The city of the branches."

"Well," Jack said, looking at Diane, "I guess our mission has begun."

"It would appear so," Diane replied. "So, what's our next move, chief?" Jack asked Brady. The old man just shrugged. "Beats the hell out of me," he said. "What do you mean?" Jack snapped, "you're supposed to be our *guide*. A guide *helps*."

"Whoa! Take it easy!" Brady said, throwing his arms up, as if to protect himself, "I don't have all the answers. But I promise, whatever I *can* do, I *will* do. You're gonna have to figure most of this out for yourself. One thing I can tell you; you ain't gonna get out by going around in circles."

"Well, I could have told you that!" Jack snapped. He turned back around, facing the road again, with his hands on the wheel. "All right," he said, "If we're gonna get out, we're gonna have to do it ourselves; he's useless."

And he started driving, this time passing the turn for Decatur and going straight. "Forget getting back onto 55," he said, "Let's just get out of this little circle of hell." He drove some more. About a mile up, he made a right. He came to a dead end which offered him only one option—to turn right again, which was back the way they came. "Damn it!" he snarled, as they headed back toward the circle they were trying to escape. Before long he was back on the C shaped bend that led straight back to Chambers Bridge.

By this time the branches were everywhere, draping the road like a curtain. He had to drive right through them, snapping them as he plowed along. "There's no way out!" Jack growled. Furious, he floored the gas, slamming through the branches as he sped recklessly forward, trying to find a different route. "Jack, please!" Diane shouted, "This isn't helping!"

But he ignored her, plowing forward the way he had just come, breaking through the branches. This time he took a different route, turning this way and that, in the vain hope that eventually they would emerge out of this dense nightmare forest and back into the real world out of which they came. But not only did that not happen; they actually found themselves back where they had started—on Chambers Bridge Road—flanked on both sides by dense mist, shrouded in darkness, and lost in a forest of fast multiplying branches.

Jack stopped the car, defeated. But the slapping sound of the branches against the car did not stop. With horror, Jack realized why: the branches had come alive. They were attacking the car, trying to get at them. "We better get off the road," Jack said. Diane agreed. So did Brady. They flung the doors open, covered their faces as best they could against the flailing branches, and darted through the mini-forest and onto the grass. Diane put Smokey down on the ground. She growled softly, looking around at her strange surroundings with a mixture of awe and fright. They were standing on a swath of empty grassland, with a marsh off to their left and the old house just up ahead, about midway between the marshes and the road. Beside the house

53

stood a shed. "Now what?" Jack asked, directing the question to no-one in particular, although he thought it would have been really nice if Brady had some answers right about now. The old man just shrugged his shoulders and said, "Damned if I know." The three just stood there, watching the trees devour their car. They had gotten out just in time; by now they would have been suffocating beneath an avalanche of bark and wood.

Then Jack noticed something—a strange stirring from within the midst of the branches, as if something inside of them was trying to break free. A branch, in the shape of an arm, forced its way out. Then another one. Diane and Brady followed Jack's gaze and watched with him as a creature, made entirely of branches, emerged out of the forest that used to be a road. And there it stood, on the side of the road, looking this way and that, it's knees bent slightly, it's arms spread, as if ready to spring into action. Jack wished he had his glock right now, but it was in his back pack, which was in the trunk of Diane's car. And there was no getting back there. The creature looked at them and bent down at the waist, as if ready to pounce. Jack braced himself, preparing to fight. Exactly how you fought something made entirely of wood, bark, and sapling, he did not know, but he would have to try.

The creature dashed straight at them. Jack stepped forward to meet it and they crashed to the ground, rolling, first with one on top, then the other, as they struggled for position. Jack wound up on top as Brady and Diane surrounded them, poised to jump in. As he straddled the creature, Jack pondered his next move. How do you kill a tree?

"Hold him there!" Diane yelled, and dashed for the shed. Moments later she emerged with an axe in her hand. "Hold it still!" she commanded, raising the axe over the creatures' legs while Jack struggled to keep the struggling tree-thing from breaking free. She brought the axe down hard, cutting most of its left leg off at the knee. It shrieked in agony as the blade went through. She raised it again, bringing it down even harder this time, and severing the lower leg completely. Again, the thing shrieked in agony. She drew back, holding the axe long ways across the front of her body. Jack released the creature, leaving it to writhe around in the grass. With only one leg, it would not be a threat.

"Are there more weapons in the shed?" Jack asked. "Yeah, come on," Diane said, leading the way. "What about the door? Does it open?" Jack asked, trying the front door of the spooky old home. It was locked.

They went into the shed, where an assortment of tools hung from the wall on hooks. More were scattered on the floor, on a work table, and on benches. When they emerged from the shed, Jack had a machete in his hand, and Grady a chain saw. And from the looks of things, just in time, as more creatures were emerging from the "forest"—in fact, a whole army of them. Actually, they were not so much emerging from the forest as the forest was *turning into* these creatures, and coming after them, having failed to destroy them in their previous form.

Using their weapons as best they could, they confronted the swarm of tree creatures, cutting into them with all their might. One after another fell before their blades, their shrieks filling the air, as they went crashing to the grass, leaving one or more of their limbs behind. But the sheer number of the creatures, as they poured forth, one after another, from the forest, was more than they could handle. They needed another plan. Jack dashed for the house again, trying the door knob. It wouldn't open. He stepped back, and with all his might he kicked the doorknob. The door flew open. "In here—fast!" he yelled to his two partners, who were on the verge of being overcome by the creatures.

They ran in and slammed the door shut. Then, moving with lightning speed, they pushed as many things as possible up against it. A sofa, two chairs, three end tables, and a chest. Then they ran for the basement. As they hurried down the steps they could hear the creatures breaking the windows. Jack knew this was not an escape. But it could buy them some time. A *very* little time, but some. Time to think. And that's all he wanted.

The basement was dark and dank, filled with old relics. On one wall was an old washer and dryer next to a basin sink. On another was a series of trunks and cases, all piled on top of each other. On the other two were the furnace, a water heater, and more relics, strewn about with no particular rhyme or reason.

"Okay," Jack said, grabbing Brady by the shoulders "What the fuck is going on and how do we stop it?" Even as he spoke he could hear the creatures crashing through the house. They would have about a minute at best, and then they would be overrun. "Circles!" Diane shouted suddenly. "What?" Jack asked. She pointed at Brady. "Maybe he already *told* us the answer. What did he say? . . . You're not gonna do it by going around in circles?"

"Yes, that's right!" Brady said, seemingly relieved that Diane was defending him. "Okay, so what?" Jack asked, as Diane frantically fiddled with her cell phone, looking something up on the internet. "Circles, circles, circles," she repeated. "What do we usually mean when we say we're going around in circles?"

"It means we're doing the same thing over and over again."

"Right!" Diane said. "But it's not about a physical pattern, or path that we follow. It's about our thoughts. Our minds go around in circles. Our thoughts. Our *branches* of thought!"

"Yes, yes!" Brady implored, certain that she was onto the answer. Or perhaps just hoping she was.

"I don't understand," Jack said, peering over Diane's shoulder as she googled the term 'branches of thought'.

And then they heard it. The sound of the basement door being broken off its hinges. It came flying down the stairs and crashed into the wall. But it was not the creatures that followed behind. Instead what came snaking down the stairs was a massive, moving forest of thin, interlinked branches, all moving furiously about. And as it moved, it grew, multiplying exponentially, with two branches becoming four, then the four eight, and so on, as it converged upon them.

"God, please hurry," Jack said as the three of them huddled together in a corner, watching as the expanding mass of branches inched forward. Diane read frantically the words that appeared on the tiny screen before her: *"Neurobiologists have gained new insights into how neurons control growth of the intricate tracery of BRANCHES called dendrites that enable them to connect with their neighbors. Dendritic connections are the basic receiving stations by which neurons form the signaling networks that constitute the brain's circuitry."*

She showed Jack the picture on the screen. The dendrites looked like the branches of a tree. Indeed, they looked like a *forest* of branches. "Our thoughts caused all of this," Diane said. "We were going in circles in our *thoughts*, worrying, *multiplying* our bad thoughts. That's what these branches are—our own thoughts!"

"Yes, yes," Brady cheered, placing his hands on her shoulders, "She's right. It was all in your minds! All of it!"

And at that very moment, the branches, literally inches away, and straining to reach them, suddenly stopped, and then, very slowly, started to recede. They watched in amazement as the floating forest slowly moved backwards back up the stairs, out the door, and out of sight, returning to whence it had come.

The three hugged in celebration, then made their way up the stairs, into the living room of the old home. They moved the furniture away from the door and went back outside. It was light out again. The road was empty of everything except their car, which sat, undamaged, on the side of the road. There was no mist on the ground, no tree creatures, and no branches, except those which hung naturally from the trees that lined Chambers Bridge Road. All was quiet and as it should be. On the grass, where they had encountered the first tree creature, was Smokey, sitting there staring at them as they approached.

"Well," Brady said, "You made it through your first city—the land of the branches. "Congratulations." He extended a hand first to Jack and then to Diane. "You mean we have to do this six more fucking times?" Jack said. Brady shrugged and said, "I don't make the rules."

"Well, maybe they get easier as we go along, right?" Diane said hopefully. "Actually," Brady said sheepishly "They get harder."

"Oh, fuck!" Jack snarled. His relief at escaping certain death was instantly replaced by the dread of having to face it six more times. "So, what's the next city?" Jack asked. "Beats me," Brady shrugged. "I was only your guide for this one. You'll be given a different guide for each city. Can't guarantee they'll be as handsome as me, but I'm sure they'll get you through."

And with that he started down the road. "Hey, wait," Jack called after him. "Just like that, you're leaving? Can't we give you a lift somewhere?"

"Not to where I'm going," he said, and winked. Then he kept going, his white trench coat billowing ever so slightly in the summer breeze.

They got back in the car. Diane took the wheel. Smokey took her seat in back. Diane drove to Decatur, turned right, then took the exit back onto 55. This time it worked fine.

16

Jack noticed a curious thing as they drove along I 55. According to his watch, which read 5 A.M., virtually no time had elapsed during the events that just occurred in the City of the Branches. It had all happened in their minds, in no time flat, or, perhaps, over a matter of minutes or seconds. Interesting. He thought about mentioning it to Diane but decided against it. Truth was he didn't want to think about it anymore. At least not right now. Instead he said, "I'm starving; how about you?"

"I'm pretty hungry too," she said. "Engaging in mortal combat with homicidal tree people really works up an appetite."

"Yeah," he said. "It sure does."

"I'll stop somewhere," she said. "Tell me when you see an exit sign." After their last experience with exit signs, Jack almost wanted to say, "Never mind, let's just go straight." Instead he said, "Okay." Moments later he spotted a sign for a rest stop, along with a McDonalds logo. "There's a place," he said. "Do you like McDonald's?"

"I love McDonald's," Diane said. "Especially their breakfasts."

"Me too," Jack said. Moments later they pulled into the restaurant. Jack checked in back. Smokey was lounging comfortably on the back seat, licking its front leg. "I guess we'll have to get it to go," he said, "Smokey's awake."

"Good enough for me," Diane said. Then she pulled up to the intercom and ordered the number 2, which was an egg sandwich with bacon and an orange juice. Jack ordered the same thing. They ate as they drove.

An hour's way up route 55 they took exit 290A to get onto I 44 West, where, according to the map Jack had finally decided to consult, they would be traveling for about one thousand miles to the Kilpatrick Turnpike West. Disneyland might be a long drive, Jack thought, but at least it was a straight one. "Let me know if you want to switch," Jack said. He thought Diane was looking tired. "I'm good," she said.

"So, are we still going to Disneyland?" Jack asked.

"Of course; why wouldn't we?" Diane replied.

"I don't know," Jack said. "Now that our mission has officially begun, I thought maybe that changed something."

"Not for me it didn't," Diane said confidently.

"That sure was weird," Jack said.

"And scary," Diane agreed.

"Yeah," Jack said, "Weird and scary. I hope they're not all like that."

"Yeah, me too," Diane said. She didn't really seem to want to discuss it, which bothered Jack, because he thought they should. But Jack was discovering that Diane didn't do much talking. She was a woman of few words. A woman of action, not words. Like the way she decoded the allegorical maze they were trapped in and found the way out. She was strong, resourceful, and smart as a whip. He was not glad to be on this mission, but if he had to be on it, he was glad he had her with him. He wondered if she felt the same way about him.

"Are you sure you don't want me to drive?" he asked again. He hated to be a nag, but she really was looking tired. *Very* tired. "In another ten minutes," she said, to his relief. "I am getting tired," she said.

"Okay," Jack replied.

A few minutes passed, and Diane said, "It's so incredible."

"What is?" Jack asked.

"Life," Diane said simply. "I mean . . . a few hours ago we were living together in my apartment, working for Manus Manufacturing, and now we are on our way to Disneyland and officially embarked on a journey to save humanity."

"It's been a busy few hours," Jack agreed. Diane just chuckled. Suddenly he had this urge to reach out and touch her knee. Just put his hand there for a few seconds, maybe even rub it a little—just to see how she reacted. He really had no idea how she would. None whatsoever. He supposed that could be attributed to two things; firstly, how close to her vest she kept things, and second, how unintuitive he was. In that respect, he was like most men. Women could read men, but men couldn't return the favor.

As he sat there pondering that thought, Diane suddenly started slouching down in her seat, as if she had feinted. But Jack quickly realized that she hadn't feinted; she had fallen asleep. Just like that; she was out. He knew she looked tired, but he didn't think she was *that* tired. Her foot had slipped off the gas, and her hands off the wheel, causing the car to slow to a near halt and career sideways. He didn't even have the chance to shout before he heard the massive foghorn blast of a tractor trailer horn and the deafening thud of the impact. Then everything went black.

Only seconds after impact Diane found herself floating. It wasn't a bad feeling; it wasn't a good feeling—it was just . . . floating. She couldn't say where she was, or where she was going. She just . . . was.

And then she was ten again, back in Reddington, P.A., outside the trailer home of her foster parents, Daniel and Susan Miller. Her dad was inside, sleeping. Her mom was out shopping. The gas can was on the ground; she had already doused the trailer, and the match was in her hand. Her hand trembled as she prepared to light it.

She never did understand why she hated her foster dad so much. Yes, she hated the things he did to her, but he told her *all* dads did those things; it was no big deal. But those things made her feel weak and scared and ashamed, and she couldn't stand it anymore. There was something wrong with her, she knew. Her father was not a bad man. In every other way, he treated her good—like a little princess. Bought her things, took her places, gave her whatever she wanted. It was just that one thing. That was all.

But that was enough. She lit the match and threw it against the wall of the trailer. Within seconds the trailer was consumed. She could hear her father screaming. He was screaming at the top of his lungs. It was the most awful sound she had ever heard. God, she wished she could have done something to save him. She was the worst little girl in the whole world. But there was nothing she could do. She watched the trailer burn. When she was sure her dad was dead, she ran crying to a neighbor for help, saying she found the trailer like that. How it happened she had no idea.

Diane wasn't floating anymore, and she wasn't ten. She was a grown woman, lying on a gurney, being rushed through a pair of doors into the emergency room. All she could feel was the terrible pain of the burns all over her body, as if someone had covered her entire body with a red-hot blanket. She screamed with pain. "We have to prep her for surgery," the ER nurse shouted. She looked around her, panic stricken. Jack was on a gurney next to her, his body broken and mangled, as doctors and nurses huddled around him, tending to his twisted frame. She only vaguely remembered who he was—a man she knew. Thought she knew.

But she didn't know anything. She did not remember the accident, or how she got here. All she knew were two things: fear and pain, and she didn't know which one was worse. They had slid the gurney beneath a tray full of instruments—needles, syringes, scalpels—all which stared her in the face as a bright light from above beat down into her eyes, and everywhere around her doctors and nurses scrambled about, poking her, rubbing her with alcohol, pulling off her clothes, all the while shouting instructions to each other in obtuse medical jargon that she did not understand.

All she knew was she hurt badly, so, so badly, like nothing she ever felt before, and they were running all around her, jabbing and poking and rubbing and shouting, while the lights were flashing in her eyes, until she couldn't stand another second of it. She began to scream.

They pounced on her, holding her down, as she writhed like a wounded animal beneath them. Above her a ring of masked faces looked down intently, as if she were a lab rat in some kind of horrible experiment. She writhed and writhed, but she could not break their grips; their hands were like iron, clamping her down to the gurney. And then they put the mask on her face. She smelled something awful, some thick, gaseous stench, and then she was breathing it in, sucking it down her throat, into her lungs, unable to move or resist. And then she was out.

⤙

Only seconds after impact Jack found himself floating. It wasn't a bad feeling; it wasn't a good feeling—it was just . . . floating. He couldn't say where he was, or where he was going. He just . . . was.

And then he was sixteen again, back in Brick, N.J., out on the lake with Sally Sanders. She had just fallen in the lake and he was sitting there, looking at her over the side of the boat, drunk as a skunk, as she flailed wildly, blood trickling down the front of her face. He had promised her he would not go out too deep, but he had. He had promised her he was not too drunk to steer the boat, but he was. And when he crashed it into a reef she pitched forward, cutting her head along the way, as she went crashing into the lake. He knew she couldn't swim, but he was almost too drunk to even comprehend the significance of that fact, as he sat there, like a stoner at a Grateful Dead concert, watching the show. And by the time the circuitry of his brain started to register the full import of what was really happening, it was too late. Almost. She was still alive, but going down for the third and final time, when he reached out his hand for her. And watched her sink, her mouth opened in a frozen scream, with bubbles coming out of it, as she disappeared from sight down into the lake.

Jack wasn't floating anymore, and he wasn't sixteen. He was a grown man, lying on a gurney, being rushed through a pair of doors into the emergency room. All he could feel was the terrible pain of the crushed bones and severed tendons in his body. He screamed with pain. "We have to prep him for surgery," the ER nurse shouted. He looked around, panic stricken. Diane was on a gurney next to him, her body broken and burned, as doctors and nurses huddled around her, tending to her burns. He only vaguely remembered who she was—a girl he knew. Thought he knew.

But he didn't know anything. He did not remember the accident, or how he got here. All he knew were two things: fear and pain, and he didn't know which one was worse. They had slid the gurney beneath a tray full of instruments—needles, syringes, scalpels—all which stared him in the face as a bright light from above beat down into his eyes, and everywhere around him doctors and nurses scrambled around, poking him, rubbing him with alcohol, pulling off his cloths, all the while shouting instructions to each other in obtuse medical jargon that he did not understand.

All he knew was he hurt badly, so, so badly, like nothing he ever felt before, and they were running all around him, jabbing and poking and rubbing and shouting, while the lights were flashing in his eyes, until he couldn't stand another second of it. He began to scream. They pounced on him, holding him down, as he writhed like a wounded animal beneath them. Above him a ring of masked faces looked down intently, as if he were a lab rat in some kind of horrible experiment. He writhed and writhed, but he could not break their grips; their hands were like iron, clamping him down to the gurney. And then they put the mask on his face. He smelled something awful, some thick, gaseous stench, and then he was breathing it in, sucking it down his throat, into his lungs, unable to move or resist. And then he was out.

⤳

When Diane woke up, she was on a bed, hooked up to monitors, with an IV drip in her arm. On either side of her were partially drawn curtains, and beyond them, other patients in other beds. She guessed she was in Post Op, recovering from whatever it is they had to do to her. Her body was wrapped in gauze, and on her hands were two loose fitting white gloves, which were secured to her wrists with bandages. The last thing she could remember was being in exquisite pain, surrounded by medical personnel, in the emergency room. The pain had subsided a great deal. For that she was grateful. But it was still there, that feeling of hot blankets pressing against her skin. But besides that, and a slight headache, she did not feel that horrible.

She tried to remember what had happened. How she wound up here. It came back to her in pieces, and not all of them fit together. She had been driving with Jack. Driving along the highway. Where she was going, and why she could not remember. And she could summon only a dim recollection of who Jack was, and why the two of them were together. Those details, she supposed, would come back to her. For now, though, maybe *not* remembering was better.

A young man in blue scrubs pulled back the curtain and came in. "I see you're awake; that's a good thing," he said, grabbing a chart from her front bed rail and looking at it. He wore a name tag that read Nurse Taylor.

"I guess," she replied.

"You guess?" the man said in an admonishing tone "You have to be more positive, Miss Foster. You're lucky to be alive after the accident you had."

"Was anyone else hurt?" she asked. "Is Jack okay?"

"Jack is here, on the other side of the hospital," Taylor said. "He sustained some injuries, but he'll be fine. He's in good hands. And the driver of the truck suffered no injuries."

"The truck?" Diane asked.

"Oh yeah," Taylor said, standing at the head of her bed and looking at her intently, "You were hit by a five-ton tractor trailer."

"Holy shit," she said. She closed her eyes and took a deep breath as the memory of the last moments before the crash came drifting back. "I was tired," she said. "I was so tired, and I just kept . . . driving. It was my fault." She looked at the nurse, horrified at the thought, and repeated "It was my fault. I could have gotten Jack killed. And the driver of that truck. And God knows how many other people."

"Coulda, woulda, shoulda," Taylor said, impatiently tapping the chart with his fingers, "But you *didn't*. Like I said, Jack will be fine, the driver's fine, and *you* will be fine, too." He gave her a scolding look that dared her to say anything else bad. "But still," she said, "look at what I've . . ."

"Uh . . . Uh," he said, silencing her with an upraised hand, "No more of that. Now, here's the plan. You've suffered third, fourth, and a few fifth degree burns on more than half of your body. You've been covered in silver sulfadiazine, wrapped in gauze, and given pain killers. But you're going to need a skin graft, and the sooner the better. The surgery is scheduled for eight A.M.—one hour from now. Dr. Miller will be performing the surgery; he's the best. Trust me; you're going to be fine."

"I guess I have no choice," she said.

"No good ones," Taylor answered. "And one more thing," he said, leaning forward until his face was only inches from hers. "You have to let go of that guilt. It will kill you." Then he straightened up, gave her a wink, and strolled off.

The next hour was a blur of nurses, technicians, and orderlies passing in and out of the room, checking her vitals, adjusting the IV, shooting her with drugs, and asking questions. Taylor—the only one of the bunch she liked—did not return. When the clock struck eight, a team of nurses came in, unhooked her from the IV and the monitor, and lifted her onto a gurney. From there a single nurse, with a mask on her face, took over and wheeled her out into the hallway, to the elevators. She pressed the button and waited, hands resting on the gurney, as the doors opened. Diane stared up at the ceiling as the elevator made a ringing noise, then started to climb. There was no-one else there, just her and the nurse, and she started to feel strange, as the drugs coursed through her veins and her heart started beating faster. She had not had surgery since she was a kid—a tonsillectomy—and she was nervous.

The doors opened, and the nurse pushed the gurney out and began taking her down a long hallway. As she looked up at the nurse, her mouth hidden by the mask, she felt an odd sense of familiarity with this woman. She knew her from somewhere. The shape of her face, the look in her eyes, the cut of her hair; it was all very familiar. *Or maybe you're imagining things,* she thought. *Maybe this whole thing is a dream.*

But no. She wasn't imagining things, and this wasn't a dream. The nurse turned a corner and headed down another hallway. The lights overhead flew by, like cars on the highway, as they moved along at an increasingly fast clip. Another turn. Another hallway. More overhead lights flying by. The nurse seemed to be in a hurry, and the further they went, the more isolated, the quieter thing got, as if they were heading into some secluded, private wing of the hospital.

Something wasn't right. She just *had* surgery; why another one so soon? And she was no doctor, but she had never heard of an emergency skin graft. Why couldn't it wait? No, none of this made sense.

The nurse turned again, this time so fast that it almost sent Diane spilling off the gurney. Diane looked up at her face. There was no hint of emotion, nothing in her eyes but steely resolve. Why wasn't she saying anything? And why was she the only one? Weren't patients usually accompanied to surgery by a *team* of medical personnel?

Diane decided to speak, if for no other reason than to calm her nerves. "You look familiar," she said. The nurse said nothing. Just kept moving along at her brisk pace. Diane wondered if maybe the nurse had not heard her. Perhaps her voice was too weak, or perhaps the nurse was just so focused on the task at hand that the words did not register. She tried again, this time louder. "Don't I know you?" The nurse looked down at her, and slowly brought the gurney to a stop. Then she lowered the mask, revealing her face. Diane's eyes opened wide in shock. She did know this woman; it was Susan Miller—her former foster parent, the widow of the man she had killed. "It's me, hon," Susan whispered with a smile. "I didn't want you to know; I thought it might . . . creep you out."

Dumfounded, Diane groped for words. "How could you . . . I mean . . . ?"

"I became a nurse after your father . . . died," Susan said. "And here I am."

Diane's mind wandered back to the aftermath of the incident. Her mother did not point the finger at her. She told the authorities that her husband was smoking in bed. They may not have believed it, but they accepted it. That's because the people involved were trailer trash, and no-one cared to investigate.

"I always felt bad about it," Susan continued. "You were just a little girl. Oh, well. At least we both landed on our feet. We can talk more later. Right now, we have to get you to surgery." With that she continued wheeling the gurney, pushing it with greater and greater speed down a twisting maze of corridors that grew progressively quieter, darker, and more remote as they went along.

Diane was flat out frightened now. She still held out a remote hope that the more bizarre elements of this episode might be attributable to the fog of drugs she was under, but that hope was diminishing with each passing second. The more likely explanation was that something here was *very* wrong. The thought was interrupted by the presence of another figure at the side of her gurney—the figure of a man. He had popped out from a room in the corridor, and was now racing down the hall with them, positioned by the side of the gurney, one hand on the rail. "Hi, Dr.," the nurse said. "Hello, Nurse Miller," he answered, "How's our patient doing?"

"Very well," she answered. Diane stared with horror at the red patchy discoloration that marked the side of the doctors' face and neck. They were burn marks. Then she remembered the nurses' words "the surgery will be performed by Dr. Miller" and she knew. She knew who was under that mask. Her suspicions were confirmed when the doctor looked down at her from over his shoulder and smiled, revealing the burned visage of her father.

〜

Jack emerged slowly from the fog of anesthesia, feeling thick and heavy and weak. His head throbbed slightly and there was a feint ringing in his ears. His vision was blurry at first, but quickly cleared. He was lying on a bed in a hospital gown. There was a cast on his left arm, and the top of his head was wrapped. There were large bandages on his torso and legs. He was hooked up to a monitor and an IV drip. On either side of him were partially drawn curtains. When he tried to move a wave of pain shot through his back and sides. On the bed, wrapped around the rail, was a beeper. He picked it up and pressed it. Moments later a nurse in blue scrubs came in. "Mr. Horn, I see your awake," she said.

"Yeah," he said. "What happened?"

"You were in a car wreck. A truck slammed into your car on the highway."

"Holy shit," Jack said, as his memory came flooding back. "How is Diane?" he asked.

"Diane's fine, she's at the other end of the hospital. She suffered a few minor injuries."

"I'd like to see her."

"Give it a few days and then you can see her. First let's get you fixed up, okay?"

"Okay," Jack said. "How long will that be?"

"Well, you've suffered some injuries, as you can see, but nothing too severe. You should be out in a week. One of our technicians is going to be by in a few minutes to take you for some X rays; that will give us a better idea of where we stand."

"Okay," Jack said, as the nurse strolled off.

Jack tried to recall what had happened, but it was mostly a fog. He remembered only bits and pieces, the way you remembered the events of a dream. They were on the highway. Diane was driving. And then . . . something. That was all he remembered.

He dug his right hand into the mattress and tried to push himself into a more upright position. A sharp pain shot through his back, but he managed to move up a few inches. Wincing, he used his butt muscles to wiggle himself back and forth, until he felt more comfortable. He closed his eyes and breathed deeply, trying to remember more. He remembered Diane, but exactly who she was, how they met, and what they were doing remained unclear. He could recall pieces—a Manufacturing plant, a basement apartment, a cat—but how it all fit together he didn't know. He could remember Diane, though. Clearly. He knew this girl, who had been a fixture in his dreams for years, was now a part of his life. That much he knew, and for now, it was enough.

Moments later, the curtains flew back and a young woman, about his age, stood at the foot of the bed, her hands clasping the handles of a wheelchair. She had a pretty face, with thin, delicate features, and it looked familiar to him. "Okay, we're gonna get you some X rays now," she said, folding down his bedrails and placing a hand behind his neck. He could smell the perfume on her neck as her long black hair spilled down onto his cast. Bit by bit, with expert precision, she maneuvered him off the bed and onto the wheelchair. Somehow, she had managed the whole thing without causing him any undue pain. "Okay," she said, "let's get you to X ray."

With that, she wheeled him out into the hallway, to the elevators. She pressed 3. The elevator made a ringing noise as the doors closed. Two floors down the doors opened and she began pushing him down a long corridor. She moved quickly, without speaking. As she pushed him along, Jack rummaged through the scattered files of his addled brain to try and remember where he had seen her before.

She turned down another corridor, her pace quickening. She seemed to be in a hurry. Why he could only imagine. It was an X ray, not an appendectomy; there was hardly any urgency here. But with each step she seemed to move a little quicker. That seemed odd to him. It wasn't the only thing that seemed odd: the farther they went, the quieter things got, as if they were moving into some remote, rarely used wing of the hospital. And not only that—it was getting darker too.

She turned down another corridor, this time so sharply that Jack winced in pain. He expected a courtesy apology, but she said nothing—just kept racing along, navigating through the corridors like a race car driver speeding down the track, with each new bend leading to a darker and more remote corridor, until Jack felt like they were no longer in the hospital at all anymore, but in some far-off place that had nothing to do with medical science.

That's when it hit him. He remembered where he had seen that face before. He had seen it six years ago, when it was younger and thinner and still not fully matured. But it was the same face, nonetheless. It was the face of Sally Sanders—the girl he had allowed to drown six years ago.

⌐

Diane almost screamed when she saw the fire ravaged face of her dead foster father smiling down at her as she lay there on the gurney, being pushed down the endless succession of darkening corridors by her former foster mother, Susan Miller. "How you doing, hon?" Daniel Miller asked. Diane wanted to leap off the gurney and flee, but she was too weak. She could barely move. "Don't be afraid," Susan said, "It's just your father. He's a doctor now."

They turned another corner, into another corridor, but this one was different. It was dark; a string of bare light bulbs overhead provided the only illumination. It was filthy, too, like the corridor of a burned out building, and the thin plaster walls, filled with holes and covered with graffiti, were crawling with cobwebs and insects. Everywhere words were scrawled out in red letters like the kind you would see on bathroom stalls. This was not a hospital anymore; it was hell!

"Don't worry, we're almost there," Susan said, and started slowing down as they approached a large black door at the end of the hallway. On it was scrawled, in bright red magic marker: *skin grafts*. Daniel fished a set of keys out of his pocket and held them up, looking for the right one. "Here we go," he said, and opened the door. He entered, and Susan wheeled Diane into the room. It was a small room with no windows and black walls. Along the walls were counters, a sink, and a variety of instruments laid out on cloths. In the center was a large black table. Next to it was a control panel with a row of dials. "Now," Daniel said, taking a pair of scrubs off a hook on the wall and sliding into them, "Let me explain what we're going to do."

Diane tried to move, but she was frozen by the drugs. It was all she could do just to flail her arms a bit. "Now, take it easy," Susan said, putting a hand on her shoulder. "Your father's going to explain the procedure."

"Thank you," Daniel said. "We're going to place you on this table. Now just beneath the surface of the table are elements, not unlike those of a stove. And these dials . . ." He placed a hand on one of the dials on the control panel. "These dials regulate the heat coming out of the elements. You see to do a skin graft, you have to get rid of the old skin and replace it with new skin. You *graft* the new skin on, understand?" He paused, smiling a small, sickly smile that revealed two rows of uneven yellow teeth. "You see this old skin you've got . . ." He opened her hospital gown and ran his hand over her skin. "This skin's no good anymore. We've gotta burn it off." And then he looked at Susan and said, "All right, let's do it." They removed her gown and the gauze on her body and then hoisted her naked frame onto the table and strapped her in. Daniel stared at her with satisfaction and said, "All right, we're ready." Susan stood at the head of the table, a hand on Diane's forehead, as Daniel fiddled with the knobs on the control panel.

Within seconds, Diane could feel the table heating up. "Please, please don't do this," she begged. "I never wanted to kill you. I just . . . I just didn't know what to do! I was just a little girl."

"Oh, that's okay, honey," Daniel said. "I understand. You just did what you had to do. And now I'm doing what *I* have to do." With that he turned the dial again and the heat intensified some more. Diane winced with pain. "Please, no," she cried. "I was just a little girl. I've had to live with what I did every day for the last twelve years. Every *minute* of the last ten years. Every *second*. I carried it with me every step I took. *Every single step!*" As she spoke those words, a wave of anger, unlike anything she had ever felt before, tore like a tornado through her body, filling her every nerve with rage. *That piece of shit had ruined her life!* And suddenly she felt nothing but rage. All of the guilt was gone. All of it. In an instant. And in that instant, something happened. The picture blinked. Everything around her sputtered, like a film that was starting to fade. And when that happened her father fell backward, bumping into the counter, with a worried look on his face. That's when Diane remembered Taylor's words: *You've gotta let go of that guilt. It will* kill *you.*

Kill you. That's exactly what was happening. The figures from her past, that she had allowed to torment her for all these years, were now *killing* her. And with that realization, the spell was broken. She broke off her restraints like they were tissue paper, and sat up straight on the table, glaring angrily at her father, who recoiled in fear under her glare. "No!" he cried, looking over helplessly at Susan, who just stared back helplessly. "Yes!" Diane said, leaping off the table. She slipped her gown back on and moved toward Daniel, who began slinking to the ground in terror. Then she said in a calm and even tone "You don't even exist." And beneath a hail of shrieks and screams, he faded away, bit by bit, into nothing. Then she turned her gaze at her mother, who raised her hands and cried "I was just trying to protect you!"

"You *should* have protected me," she snarled. "But you didn't. Now *you* don't exist either." And moments later, she didn't.

As Sally Sanders pushed Jack down the corridors, he began to realize they were not in a hospital anymore. Where they were he didn't know, but it was not a hospital. It was dark; a string of bare light bulbs overhead provided the only illumination. It was filthy, too, like the corridor of a burned out building, and the thin plaster walls, filled with holes and covered with graffiti, were crawling with cobwebs and insects. Everywhere words were scrawled out in red letters like the kind you would see on bathroom stalls. This was not a hospital anymore; it was hell!

Jack wanted to get up and run, but he knew he wouldn't get far. He was too weak and too badly injured. "Where are you taking me?" Jack asked, his heart racing. "I decided what you need is some physical therapy," she said. "Don't worry; we do it in water, so it won't hurt."

So that was it, he thought. *He drowned her; now she was going to drown him.*

She stopped at the end of the hall and fished a set of keys out of the pocket of her blue scrub pants. Then she opened the door and wheeled Jack inside. It was a small, cavernous room, with stone walls all around, and in the center a small pool filled with jet propelled, whirling water. At the foot of the pool were some steps, with rails on either side. The room was dark, with only a few bare light bulbs overhead, as if it hadn't been used for ages. Even the water looked stale and stagnant, with clusters of dirt floating around in it.

"All right," Sally said, "time to get to work." Then she wheeled Jack over to the pool steps and took off her scrubs. Underneath she was wearing a blue, one-piece swimsuit. Her body was tanned and fit looking, like he remembered it. She slapped her hands together and said "All right, up. Up!"

She hoisted Jack out of the chair, forcing him to lean on her for support. He cried out with pain. "That's all right," she said "It's supposed to hurt a little. You'll be fine." Then she started leading him down the stairs. He leaned heavily against her, barely able to support his own weight. "Please Sally," he pleaded, "Just take me back to my room!"

"Oh, you recognize me?" she said, sounding shocked.

"Of course, I do," Jack replied, "I have thought about you every day for the past six years."

"Really?" she said. "I'm surprised. And here I thought you forgot all about me the instant my cold, dead body sank down into that lake while you sat and watched me sink like a stone."

She began leading him along the edge of the pool, slowly making their way into the deeper end.

"It wasn't like that," he said. "I was drunk."

"Oh," Sally laughed. "Well, that makes it all right, doesn't it?"

"No, that's not what I meant. I mean I . . . I . . ."

"Shhh!" she said, putting a finger to his lips. "That's over now; let's just worry about getting you better."

"It's getting too deep," Jack said, as the water rose to his chin.

"No, no," she said. "It's just right."

"Please stop!" he cried, as his legs started to buckle.

"Okay," she said, and stopped. "We'll stop right here. And now I'm going to give you a little test. I want to see how long you can hold your breath under water." With that she began to release her grip on him. "No!" he cried out, grabbing for the sides. "Uh uh!" she said, pulling him back by the waist, "None of that!" She peeled him off the side and out closer to the center. Then she put her hands on his hand, looked him right in the eyes, and smiled. "Are you ready?" she asked, and then, without waiting for an answer, began to push him down.

And then he was under, thrashing wildly with his one good arm, the pain shooting through his back and legs in massive, agonizing waves as he struggled to break free. But it was no use; her grip was like iron. And then she was under with him, her hands pressing down on his shoulders, as she stared him in the face, a big smile pasted across her lips. She gave him a playful wave as she watched. He couldn't hold his breath any longer; his mouth began to open up and take in water. At that very moment she released her grip. He shot up to the surface, choking, his good arm flailing wildly. Laughing, she held him up, kicking her legs hard beneath her—hard enough to keep them both afloat. "Good job!" she said, a broad smile on her face. "That was great. How do you feel? Should we do it again?"

"Please, no!" he choked. "I . . . I . . ."

"Shhhhh!" she said, clasping a hand over his mouth. "I know. I know. You want to try it one more time." She put her hands on his head again and prepared to push him down. At that very moment the door to the pool area came flying open and Diane came running in the room, stopping at the side of the pool, only a few feet away from them. "Jack," she shouted, "Listen to me. This is all in your mind." She pointed at Sally. "*She's* all in your mind. It's your guilt. She's a figment of your imagination that you're using to torture yourself. To punish yourself. It's not real."

As Diane spoke the words, Sally seemed to fade away for a second; for a split second she seemed to get less . . . real. And instantly Jack knew Diane was telling the truth. This was all in his head. "She's crazy!" Sally snarled angrily, tightening her grip around his head. "I'll show you whose real!" She tried to push him down again, but she had less strength than before, and Jack was able to resist. "You see," Diane shouted, "She's not real."

At the sound of those words, Jack suddenly found the strength return to his body. He stood upright, on steady legs, and faced Sally. "You're not real," he said to her. She started to recoil, her hands covering her face, as Jack approached. "You're not real," he said again, and this time Sally bent over into a crouch, her hands flailing about her head, and unleashed a series of screams, each one weaker than the one before, until she simply faded out of existence.

Everything else changed too. No longer was he standing in a black, stagnant pool in a dark, cavernous room in a far-off wing of hell. Instead he was standing in a blue pool of clean water in a brightly lit room of a regular hospital. His cast had disappeared, along with his pain, and he was dressed in a pair of jeans and a T shirt.

"Congratulations," came a voice from across the pool. The owner of the voice—a young man in nurse scrubs—came strolling over, clapping his hands softly together. He had a gentle smile on his face and the name *Taylor* on his name tag. Diane gave him a hug. "Who might this be?" Jack asked. "This is—was—our guide for the second city," she said. "The one we just made it through. The city of guilt and shadows."

"I see," Jack said. Then turning his attention to Taylor, he remarked "You guides sure keep a low profile."

"That we do," Taylor agreed. "That we do." Then he turned and strolled away.

Jack walked over to Diane. They held hands and closed their eyes. Moments later, they were back in Diane's car, on the side of the road, with Smokey in the back. Jack looked at his watch. It was 6:30 A.M. No time had elapsed in the space between their arrival at the hospital and their departure.

17

ABOUT 100 MILES UP on route 44, Jack noticed a sign on the highway for Magic Mountain Amusement Park. It occurred to him that after surviving one assassination attempt, five hours of driving, and two other worldly brushes with death, that he and Diane deserved a little fun. "Do you like roller coasters?" he asked. Diane gave him a little sideways glance and, with a twinkle in her eye, said "You read my mind."

"I guess we're getting to know each other better," he said.

"Hmmm . . . I guess so," she said, with a slight twinge of suspicion in her voice, as if Jack had suggested something to which she was not quite ready to acquiesce. Her wall was still there, but now there were fissures in it. And since emerging from their last battle, she seemed different. Lighter. More open. Like a weight had been lifted from her.

A few miles up the highway, Diane got off at the exit for Magic Mountain. They pulled into the lot, got their ticket, and parked the car. "We'll have to leave Smokey in the car," Jack noted, "They don't allow pets."

"He should be okay for an hour," Diane said. "It's not too warm today, we'll just crack a window for her."

"Works for me," Jack said. They got out of the car and headed for the entrance, walking down a path lined on both sides with a dazzling array of flowers. At the entrance were giant brass arcs with signs for Magic Mountain hanging from them. They showed their tickets at the booth and entered the park. It was mostly empty. It was a large, spacious area, filled with lush plants and flower beds at various intervals, and a vast array of shops, concession stands, and rides. There was a main path that cut through the center of the park, and other, smaller ones that snaked around the rides and stands in a variety of shapes and patterns. They took the main one, passing by an assortment of game booths on either side—there were pins to be knocked down, balloons to be filled up, hoops to be filled with basketballs, and so on and so forth. From behind the counters the attendants dared them to come and try their luck. "Win a prize for the lady," shouted one; "Come on, let's see how strong that arm is," dared another. "How strong is that arm?" Diane asked, pinching his bicep. It was the first time she had actually touched him. Now Jack knew she was softening. "I don't know," he joked, "I've been through a lot in the last few days. Besides, I'm here for the roller coaster, not the games."

"Well, then let's find some roller coasters," Diane said, and they lit off, looking for the biggest coaster in the park.

As they strolled along, though, Jack had the feeling of being followed, and out of the corner of his eye he saw things that didn't sit right. People watching them. People who didn't look like they were there for the cotton candy and bumper cars. But he wasn't sure, so he said nothing. He said nothing as they went on the Ferris wheel. And the bumper cars. And the roller coaster. And the tea cups. He said nothing as they pitched soft balls at pins, tossed darts at balloons, and lobbed basketballs in hoops.

But they were there. And by the time he was sure of it, it was too late; they were closing in. By that time, he realized that Diane had noticed it, too. He looked at her, his eyes grave with concern, and said, "I think we'd better get back to the car now."

"Yeah, let's," she said simply, and they began heading down the center aisle, toward the exit. Behind them and off to their sides were men following them. They were getting closer with each step—about seven or eight in all. By the time they reached the exits, they were running. And the men were only yards behind. Then feet. And then inches. And then they were on top of them, only feet away from the curb off the street that ran along the front part of the park. "Get off of me!" Diane cried out as a large man grabbed her in a bear hug and began dragging her toward a black Sedan that was parked just yards away. "Let her go!" Jack shouted, as two men grabbed hold of him and lifted him off the ground, one of them holding his legs, one his feet. "Help!" Diane screamed, but her scream was interrupted by the thundering sound of bullets. A hail of them, directed their way, coming from a white van that screeched to a halt just yards away from them. The men released their grips on Jack and Diane as a voice from the van shouted, "Get in! Now!" Jack and Diane ran for the open door of the van and leapt inside as their attackers scrambled for cover. The door shut, and the van sped off.

There were two figures in the front seat and one in the back. All three were clad in long, flowing white robes, and their heads, and most of their faces, were covered with hoods. "Thank you, you saved our lives," Diane said. "Don't thank us yet," the driver said. "Wait until you are safe."

The man drove them down a series of side streets ending in a long, gravelly road. At the end of the road was an opening beneath an underpass. It looked like an opening to a drainage ditch; it did not seem big enough for a vehicle. But they drove straight into it, plunging them into near to- tal darkness, as they traveled through the long tunnel beneath the earth. They emerged into a wide path, lined on both sides with a lush forest of brightly colored, perfectly manicured flowers. The path led into a massive courtyard, with a red cobblestone floor, an assortment of flower beds, and trees and benches situated at regular intervals. The trees stretched half a mile into a deep blue sky, and their leafy branches formed perfect canopies against the hot August sun. Beyond the courtyard were massive stone walls, about a hundred feet high, and carved out with the finest detail. On top of the walls, stationed about twenty feet apart, were more hooded figures in white robes, with guns in their hands. In the middle of the walls were two massive wrought iron gates that curved into an arch at the top.

The driver parked the car in the middle of the courtyard, and pressed a button on the side, which opened the van doors. Diane, Jack, and the three hooded figures emerged from the van. Jack and Diane looked around, drinking in the scene with open-mouthed awe. It was gorgeous, like some- thing out of a sci-fi movie.

"Holy shit!" Jack said, observing his new surroundings.

"Where are we?" Diane asked. "This," the driver said, motioning with his hand, "is our city. Eden." And then he lowered his hood, revealing the face of a snake, perched on top of a long neck. The other two figures fol- lowed suit, lowering their hoods. "Holy shit!" Jack said again. This sight was even more impressive than the courtyard, although not by much. "I am glad you are impressed," the driver said. He extended a hand to Jack—a gnarled, scaly appendage, with only four fingers, that looked like it would be hard to employ for delicate operations—and said "My name is Crios. I am one of the city's magistrates."

"Nice to meet you," Jack said, shaking his hand. "I'm Jack. This is Diane." Crios shook hands with Diane and said, "I know who the two of you are."

"How do you know us?" Diane asked.

"My people have been waiting for you and Jack for a thousand years," he said.

"I don't understand," Diane said.

"You will," Crios replied. "In time. In time everything will be explained. But first things first. First let's get you two cleaned up and fed. You look tired and hungry."

"We are," Diane replied gratefully. "Very much so."

"Then come with me," Crios said, waving to the guards as he approached the gate. Moments later the gate opened, and they walked forward onto a wide path with a red clayish surface. Crios turned to them and said, "This path will take us to my home, where you can eat and wash up. Then I will take you to see Glycon, the high priest. He will explain everything to you." At that point the other two figures waved good bye and wandered off.

As they walked, Crios said, "Our city is laid out in a series of concentric circles. Each circle features a different aspect of the city. On the outskirts are mostly factories and warehouses. That's where we are now."

Jack looked about as they walked. The city was breathtaking, like something out of a time capsule. Even there, in the industrial section, the buildings were ornate and beautiful—marvels of craftsmanship constructed with the greatest of care. Next in the circle was the business district, and after that, residential. All featured the same dazzling construction, the same brilliant design, the same attention to detail.

They soon arrived at Crios's home, a large, but simple two-story stone structure, with massive windows in front, and a wide staircase, flanked on either side with copious amounts of trees and shrubbery, that lead up to a large, wooden door. They followed Crios up the stairs to the door, where he let them in.

"Welcome to my home," he said, motioning with his hand as they observed the interior of their snake friend's home. "It's lovely," Diane said. "Come, let me show you around," Crios replied. He showed them one room at a time: the living room, with its antique fire place, book shelves, and chaise sofa; the parlor, with its large, wooden dining table and matching server and china closet; the kitchen, with its six-burner stove, stainless steel appliances, and round oak table; the family room, with its modular seating and 60-inch flat screen TV, and then the upstairs, with three bedrooms, all tastefully decorated, with cherry colored dressers and nightstands. On one side of the hallway was one bedroom and a bathroom, on the other side were two bedrooms, one of them occupied by their host. Crios ended the tour with the bedrooms, saying "As you can see, there are two extra bedrooms. The one on the end is mine; you may choose between the other two which one you wish to share, or, if you prefer, you may have one each. I will prepare a meal for us while you get settled in. After that, you will have time for a nap and then, if you wish, I will take you to see the high priest at the temple." With that, he turned and walked down the stairs, leaving them to get settled in.

Jack looked at Diane and said, "Well, this should be interesting."

"Yeah," she agreed with a soft, almost shy smile. Regarding the sleeping arrangements, he was not going to suggest they share the same room, but neither was he going to rule it out. So, he left it up to her, saying simply: "So, how do you want to work the bedroom situation." She smiled coyly and said, "I'll take that one," pointing to the one closest to the staircase. "Okay," Jack said. With that, they went into their bedrooms.

Jack put his back pack on the bed and unpacked his stuff. Then he took a shower, threw on a pair of boxer shorts, and flopped down onto the bed. He was exhausted. This reprieve came at a good time. He needed some time to recharge his batteries. So did Diane. Within minutes he was fast asleep. He didn't dream.

He woke up a few hours later, at about two o'clock, feeling refreshed. He threw on some cloths and went across the hallway, putting an ear to Diane's door. He didn't want to wake her up if she was still sleeping. He knocked just hard enough that she would hear if she was awake, but not hard enough to wake her if she wasn't. A moment later, she opened up, a robe cinched around her body, and a towel wrapped around her hair. His heart did a little dance, and for a moment his words caught in his throat. She gave him a coy smile, as she sensed his discomfort, and again Jack got the distinct feeling that she was softening up. No doubt about it; the fissures in the wall were deepening.

"Just checking to see if you're ready for lunch," Jack said. "Getting ready," she said, her voice coy and playful. She stood in the doorway, her hands caressing the edge of the door, and one bare foot on top of the other, rubbing it back and forth, as she stared at him with those big, brown eyes. There was a small, impish smile on her face.

"Why don't you come in?" she said. If Jack's heart was dancing before, it was leaping now. "Okay," he said simply, as she opened the door for him. He walked into the room. She closed the door. For several moments they stood there, facing each other, their eyes locked, the tension building, before she put her hands on his chest and pushed him slowly toward the bed, until he fell backwards onto it. Then she began to undress him, first taking off his shoes, then his pants, then his underwear. Then she straddled him and began kissing him, first slowly and softly, then deeper, probing with her tongue. He turned her over onto her back and entered her, thrusting hard as her fresh scent filled his nostrils. When he came, he had the same sensation he had experienced in his dreams—like he was melting into her. And just as she did in the dreams, this is where she stopped him.

"Why?" he asked. "Why do we have to stop?" But she just shook her head, the way she did in the dreams, and said, "No. We mustn't." And with that, the feeling was gone, and he rolled off of her, panting, his body limp. Maybe it was good that she stopped him. He had never made love like that, never experienced such ecstasy. Anything more might have killed him.

⌒

Lunch was exquisite—eggs, bacon, three kinds of fruit, cereal, pastries, and juice. It was a meal fit for king, and they gobbled it up like two people who hadn't eaten for days. When they were finished, Crios made good on his promise to give them a tour of the city. He had arranged for a cab to pick them up.

As they waited out front they were expecting a yellow taxi, but what they got was something different—a magnificent carriage being drawn by two beautiful white horses. "I thought you might prefer it this way," Crios said, giving them a smile. "I love it!" Diane said. "Good," Crios replied. "Perhaps I will stay behind. Orion will be a more than sufficient tour guide." With that, the three of them approached the carriage. Crios leaned into the driver's compartment and said, "Good morning Orion; I trust you will give my friends here a good tour of our fair city."

"With great pleasure," Orion replied, his hands wrapped around two long cords that extended to the horse's neck and mouth. "Good," Crios said, "then I will leave them in your hands." On that note Jack and Diane climbed into the carriage. Orion pulled on the cords, and they were off. The clip clop of horse shoes provided a steady accompaniment to the tour guides' words as they roved about the city.

Like Crios had said, the city was arranged in a pattern of concentric circles, with each circle featuring a different aspect of the city. The outermost circle, or outskirts, of the city, featured mostly warehouses and factories; after that parks and recreation; after that homes; after that the business district; and after that, in the center of town, the residences of the city's high-ranking officials. Each section had its own highlights; the towering Titan Packing and Shipping plant—a three story factory that was built over three hundred years ago; the Twin Oaks Park—a sprawling patch of lush green land, filled with oak trees and flowers, with a crystal blue stream cutting through the middle; the Eden museum—a brilliant marvel of architectural genius that housed hundreds of the city's most treasured artifacts; the Malegros Palace—a two story restaurant that had been serving patrons the finest cuisine imaginable since the early sixteenth century; and so on and so forth.

As they passed each landmark, Orion filled them in on all the details, a certain pride filling his voice, as if he were personally responsible for the achievements he was highlighting. For Jack, though, the highlight of the tour was simply being there, side by side with Diane, in that quaint carriage, with the warm summer air on their skin, as they were transported through this ancient wonderland.

The entire tour took about an hour; the city was small, about ten square miles, with a population of only a few thousand. When it was over, Orion returned them to Crios's home, where the magistrate was waiting for them on the front porch. By then it was mid-afternoon.

"I hoped you enjoyed your tour," Crios said as they approached.

"We did, very much," Jack replied. "You have an amazing city, here," Diane added. "Glad you like it," Crios said, "I only hope Orion didn't bore you too much with all the details."

"Not at all; it was quite fascinating," Diane answered. Jack agreed.

"I'm glad you enjoyed yourself," Crios said. "If it is agreeable to the two of you," he went on, "I would like to bring you to see our Chief Priest; he can better explain some of the things I mentioned to you earlier." Jack and Diane exchanged a glance, and said, almost as one "Sure, we'd like that."

"Very well," Crios said, "Come with me; we shall go there now."

They followed him out into the driveway, and into a large, black Sedan. He started it up and drove them to the Great Temple, which was located in the center of town, where the residences of the higher-ranking town officials were also located. The temple was a massive stone structure, with colossal pillars, and no ceiling. Surrounding it was a sprawling courtyard, with chairs and kneelers carved out of stone.

They made their way across the courtyard, into the temple itself, where an altar sat in the middle of a large room that was filled with statues, paintings, and a wide variety of engravings. Along the sides of the room were a number of openings that led into passageways. Standing by the altar was a hunched figure wearing a black robe. He approached them slowly; he was old and walked with a limp. He carried in his hand a tray with a candle in it, which, as best they could tell, he used for light, as his vision seemed quite poor. He held the candle up to their faces, first to Jack's, then Diane's, squinting to see them clearly, then said, in a satisfied voice "Yes. Yes. Welcome, my friends."

"Thank you," they replied. He nodded his head and said, "Follow me." Then he headed toward one of the openings, which led into a narrow corridor. Along the way there were more openings that led to more corridors, as if part of a great labyrinth, which, they supposed, was befitting an ancient temple. Some ways down he turned into one of the openings. They followed him into a small room. It was dark and had no windows. Glycon lit up two lanterns that were hanging from the wall, giving the room ample illumination. In the middle was a desk and a few chairs; on one wall was a filing cabinet and on another a bookcase filled with dusty old books. Glycon invited them to sit down, which they did. Then, with his hands trembling slightly, he took a large book off the shelf, turned it to a page that had been marked with a bookmark, and began reading:

> And when the two thousand years are finished, saviors will be sent, two of them, young and strong, a man and a woman, and they will bring a great light to you, and they will stand in your holy place, and read, and you will understand, and the scales of your eyes and your heart will fall off like rain, and the curse, which was imposed at the start, will be no more. And their names will be Jack and Diane.

And with that he pointed a trembling finger at the passage he just read, poking it several times as he spoke, and said, "You are the ones who have been prophesized to lead us out of darkness."

"Well . . . we are certainly honored," Jack said, "but we know nothing about any of this. You will have to explain it to us." Glycon walked over to his desk and seated himself behind it; Diane and Jack faced him as he spoke. "Of course," he said, "I will explain. You are familiar with the story of Adam and Eve and the serpent?"

"Of course," they replied.

"Well, the serpent was cursed. That much you know. What you may not know is that this serpent had offspring. And those offspring had offspring. And so on, all the way to the present day. And those offspring were cursed with the appearance of snakes and an inability to read and understand the scriptures."

Glycon got up, hobbled back over to the bookcase, and took a large, thick bible off the shelf and held it up. Then he opened it and said "I can read in over a dozen languages, but when I try to read this book . . . nothing. It appears before my eyes as gibberish. And the same goes for all my people. We cannot read the words of this book. But it was prophesized that one day this curse would be removed. By you." He pointed at them as he spoke the last two words.

"What would we do?" Diane asked.

"Faith cometh by hearing, and hearing by the word?" Glycon said, quoting scripture. "And how can they hear *without a preacher*? You are the preachers! You have been appointed to bring us the word. To read it to us, in our temple, week after week. To explain it to us. And then the curse will be lifted, and we will be able to understand it and read it for ourselves. And our appearance will be changed, too; we will become as you—men and woman—rather than these . . . things."

He closed the bible and placed it back on the shelf. Then he simply stood and stared at them, expectantly, through those big, unblinking snake eyes, as if waiting for them to say something. When they didn't, he said, "So, will you do it? Will you stay and release us from this curse?"

"I don't suppose it can hurt to stay a few days," Diane said, looking at Jack, who instantly agreed. "Excellent!" Glycon said, "We will be forever in your debt."

"Well, you did save our lives," Jack said. "So, we are happy to repay you."

And with that Glycon blew out the lanterns, and, candle in hand, led them back down the corridor and out into the temple area, where Crios stood waiting for them. "They have agreed to help us!" Glycon said triumphantly as he approached Crios. "Wonderful!" Crios said. "We will arrange for the temple readings to begin as soon as possible, at the governor's discretion of course."

"Have they met the governor yet?" Glycon asked. "That is our next stop," Crios answered, turning toward them. "With your permission," he said, "I would like to bring you to meet Attalos, our governor. His office is only half a block from here."

"Sounds good to me," Jack said, and Diane quickly agreed. Within minutes, they were back in Crios's Sedan, on the way to the governor's office.

Crios, Jack, and Diane approached the reception desk. The female snake person behind it smiled and asked them to state their business. "We are here to see the governor; he is expecting us," Crios said. "I will notify him," she smiled. They took seats in the waiting room. It was a large room, with chairs on three walls, and more in the middle. A gorgeous glass chandelier hung from the high ceiling. There was a bookcase in one corner, and a fireplace in another. Spread neatly on coffee tables, in accordion fashion, were dozens of magazines. There was one other snake person in the room—an older looking female sitting with legs crossed, staring straight ahead, hands folded neatly across her knees. That was something Jack liked about the snake folk; they were so calm and dignified—a bit too formal, yes—but not standoffish or stuffy. In point of fact he liked them as much, if not better, than actual people.

"The governor will see you now," the woman at the desk said. "It's the second office to the left down the hallway." Crios stood behind as Jack and Diane made their way to the office.

"Welcome," the governor said, greeting them at the door to his office, "Please come in, have a seat."

There were two seats by the governors' desk; they took one each. Behind the desk was a bookcase; on one wall was a filing cabinet, and on the other, a stack of boxes, overflowing with papers. On his desk, facing them, was a framed picture of the governor with a female snake person and two little snake people, which Jack presumed to be his family. The only other things on the desk were a desk blotter, a paper weight, and some organizers.

The governor sat down behind his desk and folded his hands on the blotter. Judging by his gait and voice, Jack guessed he was middle aged, although it was hard to tell; snake people did not show their age like regular people. "I want to thank you for meeting with me," the governor said.

"No, thank you for having us," Diane interjected.

"I trust it you have enjoyed your stay so far?" he asked.

"Very much," they answered, almost as one.

"And Crios has treated you well?"

"Absolutely," Diane said, and Jack quickly agreed.

"If you are dissatisfied with any aspect of your accommodations, I want to know about it immediately," he said with an almost grave tone.

"Everything—and everyone—has been terrific," Diane said, and again Jack agreed.

"You know . . ." the governor said, his voice faltering just a bit, "The well-organized, peaceful society you see was not always like this. You spoke with Glycon; you know about the curse?"

"Yes," they said.

"Well, for centuries after the curse, there was no Eden, no city where we dwelt together. We were scattered all over the world, outsiders, hated, hunted, persecuted. Just as the bible said, we went about on our bellies, eating dust."

"Oh, that's terrible," Diane said.

"It *was* terrible," Attalos agreed. "But then, slowly, as the centuries passed, we began to find each other, forming tribes, one here one there. And then, over the course of many more centuries, we came together and united to form this city. We called it Eden in reference to our past fall and in anticipation of our future deliverance."

"That seems appropriate," Diane said.

"Yes, we thought so. The city was not always as you see it—united, peaceful, organized. For a long time, we fought amongst ourselves. There were insurrections, battles; a great deal of blood was spilled. We are a fickle bunch; it doesn't take much for us to turn on each other. It took us a long time to become the society you see before you today."

"Well, you've done an admirable job," Diane said.

"Thank you," he said, "And now to the matter at hand. I spoke with Crylon. And he informs me that you are willing to help us."

"Yes," Jack said.

"That's very kind of you. I can't tell you how much that means to our people."

"Well, you did save our lives," Jack noted.

"And Crylon informed you of what your duties would be?"

"Yes," Diane said.

"Very well," Attalos said, "Then it is settled. You will conduct regular readings at the temple. I will arrange all of the details with Crylon."

"Okay," Diane said.

"Very well, then," Attalos said, "I shall leave you in Crios's good hands now. If there is anything you need from me, please let me know immediately."

"We certainly will," Diane said. On that note, they thanked the governor and returned to Crios, who sat waiting for them in the waiting area. "I trust all went well with Attalos," Crios said, standing up. "Yes, very well," Diane said. "Excellent," Crios said, as they filed out of the building and back toward his car. As they got in he said, "There is one more thing I must show you. It is a short drive from here. The King's Palace."

It was a short drive indeed. Within a minute, they were there. They got out of the car and approached the palace. It was a massive, stone structure, perfectly round, with a dome on top, surrounded by a mote, with a drawbridge that dropped over the mote. All along the roof were guards, stationed at regular intervals. As they approached a figure came forward, meeting them at the foot of the drawbridge. "This is Dorian," Crios said. "He is the palace chief of staff."

"Glad to meet your acquaintance," Dorian said, shaking their hands. He had the same formal air as most of the snake people, only more so. "Come," he said, "I shall give you a tour." They followed. Crios stood behind.

Dorian led them across the bridge, into the lobby of the palace. The lobby featured a super high ceiling and a glistening marble floor, which led to a massive, red-carpeted staircase, about twenty feet wide, with intricately designed banisters on either side and one in the middle, which led to two more staircases, one on each side. Dorian led them up the one on the right, saying "This is the first floor—where the king's living quarters are located."

He led them down a wide, red-carpeted hallway, with many doors on either side. He opened them, one by one, and showed them what was behind each door. First was a living area: it featured a beautifully crafted space rug, surrounded on three sides by red sofas, with a glass table in the middle; on one wall was a chest flanked by a mirror; on another a vanity; on another was a wood burning fireplace, with a fantastic painting above it; and in the corner was another vanity, with a mirror. Next was the bedroom: it featured a canopy bed, with night stands and lamps on either side; in the middle of the room were two sofas with a small desk and chair behind them; scattered through the room were an assortment of lamps, vanities, and mirrors, and off in the corner a private bathroom. Next was the kitchen: it featured granite countertops, a black satin refrigerator, and an island table with three lamps hanging over it; all of the cabinets were of a sparkling cherry wood finish, and in the corner was a magnificent two door, three drawer pantry.

There was also a library, a mini-museum, a gymnasium, a sauna, a private massage room, a theatre, and a kitchen, where the king's meals were prepared. In a separate wing of the palace were the servants' quarters, which he also showed them. There were dozens of servants: gardeners, landscapers, chefs, chauffeurs, a masseuse, a nutritionist, a doctor, housekeepers, a handyman, and a veterinarian for the horses.

Next, he took them outside, where he showed them the king's tennis courts, garden, pool, and his field of horses. When the tour was finished, he turned to them and asked "Well, what do you think?"

"It's incredible!" Diane answered for the both.

"I'm glad you are pleased with your accommodations," Dorian replied. "Of course, you are free to request any changes."

"Pardon me?" Diane said. Dorian looked confused for a moment, then said, "Surely you've been told. You are the King and Queen. This is your home."

They looked at each other in disbelief, then back at Dorian. *"Our home?"* Jack said.

"Of course. I'm surprised Crios didn't mention it. I guess he wanted it to be a surprise. You are our new king and queen now, and I, Dorian, am at your service." He bowed.

"Well, what about the current king and queen?" Jack said.

"Oh, you do not understand," Dorian replied. "There is no current king and queen. We have never had a king and queen. This palace was erected entirely in anticipation of your arrival. You are the only ones that may occupy it. But don't worry; it has already been fully staffed, and all the servants are already at work, and ready to tend to your every need and desire."

"This is all so . . . sudden," Diane said. "Yes," Jack agreed, "We really weren't expecting this."

"I understand. Take your time and think about it. The palace will still be here when you have arrived at your decision. Come, let us go back to Crios."

For Jack there was no decision. He wanted to move in and live there with Diane forever. But he sensed hesitation on her part. At the very least, though, she seemed open to staying for a while, while they helped rid the snake people of their curse. They followed Dorian back around the side of the palace, and back to Crios, where he stood waiting for them in his car. They got in and he drove them back to his home. It was the last night they spent there. The next day, by mutual agreement, they moved into the King's palace.

⌒

Crios parked in front of the palace and said, "Be well, my friends. And thank you."

"Thank you," they replied together, and got out of the car. With nothing but their backpacks, they approached the palace, as Dorian lowered the drawbridge. And then they entered the great lobby of the palace, two kids who had spent their lives on the run, living in hovels and basements, sleeping in alleys and on benches, to take their place as king and queen of their own city.

They had the entire day planned. First, they would unpack the very few possessions they actually owned. Then, they would have the servants prepare them a feast for breakfast. Next, they would go to the stable and do some horseback riding. Then a few rounds of tennis. Next, lunch. Then, a walk around the palace, where they would get a better look at all the sights. Then, a workout in their private gym, followed by a swim, and then a shower. Then dinner. After that, a movie in the theatre, an evening stroll through the garden, and finally, some TV watching in their bedroom.

And that's exactly what they did. It was glorious—a life unlike anything they had ever experienced. No scrounging for money. No toiling at menial tasks for pennies. No sleeping in hovels. No watching over their backs, no running, no fear. And to top it all, they had each other's arms to fall into at night, when the day's activities were over.

The next several days followed a similar pattern, although they stepped out more often, having their chauffeur take them to a variety of restaurants, parks, theatres, playhouses, museums, and shops. They stocked their closets full of the finest apparel and wore different cloths every day.

Soon the temple readings started. The entire town would crowd into the massive temple courtyard to hear Diane read the scriptures and teach their meaning. Jack was impressed by her command of the scriptures, as were the citizens of Eden, who applauded her each time she spoke. But more than that, the curse was being lifted, just as the prophecy said it would. More and more the citizens of the town were able to read the scriptures for themselves.

And then one day, as Diane was reading in the temple, it happened. During mid-sentence she was interrupted by the sound of a great cry that filled the courtyard. It was a cry of jubilation, as the snake people were snake people no more; they had been transformed into humans. With astonishment, they stared at one another; men at women, women at men, men at men, women at women, scarcely able to believe their eyes. The curse had been lifted.

As Jack watched the scene from his front seat, his sense of jubilation was mixed with an undercurrent of dread. They had achieved what they had set out to achieve. Now what? For his part, he knew what he wanted. He wanted to live the life he was living now, which was glorious in every possible way, forever. But what would Diane want? Would she want to stay now that they had finished their business here, or would she want to leave and finish their mission?

That night they dined in relative silence. As always, dinner was exquisite—a magnificent sampling of succulence cooked up by their chef and served by their servants. After dinner they took a stroll through the garden, then retired together to their bedroom. As Jack watched television, Diane was busy on her laptop. The silence between them grew thick and awkward, until Diane finally broke it, saying simply, "So, now what?" Those three words confirmed what Jack already knew: she was thinking about leaving. "Now nothing," Jack said. "We live happily ever after."

"But what about our mission?" Diane said.

"Look, who started us on this mission?" Jack asked.

"God, of course," Diane replied.

"Right, God. So, if he wants us to finish, *when* he wants us to finish, then surely He will let us know. The same way he drove us here, he will drive us out. In the meantime, maybe He is giving us a well-deserved vacation. Why not just enjoy it?" To Jack's surprise, Diane said simply, "I guess so."

And for two weeks that was the last they spoke of it. During that time, they continued to live as they had been living. They continued sampling all of the pleasures their esteemed positions had afforded them: the succulent feasts, prepared by chefs and served by servants; the nightly strolls through their magnificent garden; the shopping sprees, where money was no object; the swims in the pool; the rounds of tennis on their own private court, with ball boys to retrieve the balls for them; the nightly movie viewing in their own theatre, with no one to disturb them, and no lines to wait on; their own private masseuse to knead their flesh like dough; the chaffer to take them anywhere they directed; the gardener to tend to their flowers and trees; the landscaper to mow their grass and trim their bushes; the vet to keep their horses happy; and the maids to keep their quarters clean and disinfected. And for two more weeks they stayed there, living as king and queen in Eden. With each day they fell deeper in love with their lives, their town, and each other, until leaving became unthinkable. Until one evening, when Diane not only thought it, but brought it up again. Like the last time they discussed the subject, they were lying in bed; Jack watching TV, Diane on her laptop. She said, out of nowhere, "What if God isn't going to make us leave? What if it's up to us?"

"What?" Jack asked, lost in his movie.

"Remember what you said: 'If God wants us to finish, *when* he wants us to finish, then surely He will let us know. The same way he drove us here, he will drive us out.'"

"I remember," Jack said, wishing Diane had not brought this up again.

"Well, what if God isn't going to make us leave? What if it's up to us?"

"Well, then so be it," Jack said, "If God is willing to give up on the mission, then it couldn't have been that important."

"But what if it was? What if it was important and God still gave us the option of giving it up if we wanted to. In fact, what if He made giving up seem especially tempting, so tempting that it would seem almost impossible *not* to give up."

"What?" Jack asked, confused.

"Think about it," Diane said, staring at him intently. "This is the land of the snake people. What do snakes do? They tempt. And what are we being tempted to do? To stay here forever and *abandon our mission*."

"Why would they care if we abandon our mission?"

"Maybe they don't. But we do."

"Huh?"

"Remember the first city? The branches?"

"Yes."

"Well, they weren't real branches. They were branches of thought, stemming out from a *tree*. Now look at this tree." Diane pointed to her computer. Jack looked. On the screen was a picture of the human nervous system.

"It's not a literal tree," Diane said, "it's our nervous system. But it looks just like a tree. What tree did Adam eat from? The tree in the *middle*. What's in the *middle* of us? Our nervous system. He *ate* from his own self; he followed his own physical cravings, his carnal nature; that's how he got kicked out of the garden. And look what is hanging from this tree—from our nervous system?"

She showed him another picture. At the top of the nervous system hung the brain. "It's our brain," Jack said.

"It's called the *reptilian* brain," Diane said, "Read this." Jack read the words Diane was pointing to. The reptilian brain/complex *"The R-complex consists of the brain stem and the cerebellum. Its purpose is closely related to actual physical survival and maintenance of the body. The cerebellum orchestrates movement. Digestion, reproduction, circulation, breathing, and the execution of the "fight or flight" response in stress are all housed in the brain stem. Because the reptilian brain is primarily concerned with physical survival, the behaviors it governs have much in common with the survival behaviors of animals. It plays a crucial role in establishing home territory, reproduction and social dominance. The overriding characteristics of R-complex behaviors are that they are automatic, have a ritualistic quality, and are highly resistant to change."*

"Don't you see?" Diane said. "The tempting snake hanging from the tree is our own brain. *We* created this temptation. We wanted out of that mission, and we created this way out. Every one of these missions is a challenge, right? Well, the challenge of *this* mission is the *temptation* to stay here forever! To successfully meet this challenge, as we did the first two, we have to resist the temptation. We have to leave!"

"I don't want to leave!" Jack said. "Leave for what? We almost *died* on our first two missions. I never experienced that much pain, that much terror, that much misery in my whole life, and I've had my share. I *never* want to go back!" He crossed his arms and lay there, a sullen look on his face, as Diane pondered her next move.

Diane waited a few minutes for him to cool off, before speaking again. "I understand how you feel," she said, putting a hand on his shoulder. "A part of me, a *big* part, doesn't want to leave, either. I mean, these have been the best two weeks of my life. But . . ." She struggled to find the words. "But the mission, Jack." She tightened her grip on his shoulder. "We have an obligation to the world. We were meant to show them the way back to the garden. How can we just abandon them?"

"I don't want to abandon anyone," Jack said, "But I don't think we should continue. I mean, think about it: What are the next four cities going to be like? Remember what Brady said, that they would get harder, not easier. Well, if it gets any harder than it has been, I can't endure it. And what if the mission fails? What if we go through another city, or another two, or three, and die? Then what? The vultures pick our bones and God finds two other saps to do his little mission."

"We can never know the future, Jack," Diane said. "We can only do what we're called to do. We can only do our best."

Jack had the sinking feeling that Diane was leaving, with or without him. And that meant he was leaving too, because he'd rather go *anywhere* with her, no matter how bad the place, than to stay behind without her, no matter how good the place. But then she said something that he didn't expect. She said, "I want to go back. I won't go without you, though; I *can't* go without you, but I wish you would agree to go with me."

Jack felt a great sense of relief. She wasn't going to make him leave. He could stay there, *they* could stay there, if he wanted to. And he wanted to. And they did. They stood. Jack thought things might be different after that. He thought Diane might be bitter, but she wasn't. In fact, she never mentioned it again; nor did anything in her demeanor suggest the slightest trace of resentment. They carried on exactly as before, enjoying all the fruits of their lofty positions: the succulent feasts, the nightly garden strolls, the shopping sprees, the swims, the tennis, the private movies, and everything else that came with being the king and queen of their own city. If anything, they enjoyed things even more now that the city was human, their fellow citizens—and subjects—looking just like them, although retaining that peculiar air of formality.

Two more weeks passed. The town was preparing for the yearly Founding Day festival that commemorated the date of the founding of the city. Every year it was a big celebration, but this year especially, for this was the thousandth-year celebration. This fact, along with the recent lifting of the ages long curse, would make this year's celebration by far the biggest of them all. And the whole town was preparing: restaurant owners were preparing Founding Day specials; liquor stores were stocking up to ten times their normal inventory; bakeries were ordering dozens of extra cakes; grocers were tripling their orders; sanitation crews were firing up dozens of extra trucks; police were marshalling extra security forces; and on and on. The whole town was bustling as the big day arrived. Events were scheduled all over town; bands playing in the town square; barbecues in the parks; fireworks in the temple courtyard, and so on. And a new festivity was added to the list; citizens would be gathering into the king's courtyard to hear him say a few words at midnight from the roof.

And so, when twelve o'clock rolled around, Jack and Diane made their way up to the roof. Jack stared down at the bustling throng of people, as they looked up expectantly. The fireworks had been set off already; the only thing left was for the king to speak. With Diane at his side, he approached the lectern that had been set up on the roof. He looked down at his subjects. "Good evening, my friends," he said, to polite applause. "How are all of you this evening?" A chorus of responses floated up at him. "Very good," he smiled, waving. "I'm glad to hear you are all having a good time. Because isn't that what it's all about for you people? Having a good time, while you huddle away together here in your little fool's paradise, hiding away from the real world? But what else would I expect? Snakes will be snakes, right? And snakes, at their core, are nothing but cowards, slithering around, causing trouble, then slithering away at the first sign of trouble." Standing at his side, Diane's eyes widened with astonishment at the sound of his words. The crowd was as silent as a tomb, their jaws hanging open as they listened in disbelief to the hateful diatribe being aimed their way. Jack continued: "You were cursed at the beginning and you are still cursed. You may look like people, but inside you remain snakes—vile, filthy, disgusting snakes, full of deceit and evil. You were snakes before, you are snakes now, and you will be snakes tomorrow, the day after, and all the days of your miserable, worthless lives. And that, my people, is all I have to say to you."

On that note, Jack turned to Diane, took her hand, and led her, running, down the stairs that led from the roof back down into the palace, as the words of Attalos flashed in his mind: *They are a fickle bunch, quick to turn on each other.*

They ran through the long hallway on the second floor, into the parlor, and sat down on the sofa. They could hear the roar of the people as they stormed the palace. Within minutes they would be inside, with the aim of tearing them apart limb by limb. Dorian came in and shouted, "They are breaking down the doors; we cannot hold them back. What has come over you? Why did you do that?"

"Leave us alone," Jack said simply. "Close the door and leave; we do not wish to be disturbed." Dorian just stood there, his mouth agape. "Go!" Jack roared. Dorian gave him one last bewildered look, then fled the room, shouting orders to the other servants as he fled down the hall.

Jack took Diane's hands in his own, looked her in the eyes, and said, "I guess we have no more reason to stay here." Diane smiled at him—a soft, sad smile full of warmth and gratitude and pride. "I guess not," she sighed. "I guess now we'll just have to return to the real world and continue our mission."

"I guess so," Jack said. They could hear the townspeople down below now, flooding into the palace, running up their stairs to the second floor. Moments later they burst through the door, a human tidal wave coming straight at them, their clenched fists raised in fury, their mouths pouring forth curses like water. But Jack and Diane didn't see them; not really. They appeared to them as phantoms, floating harmlessly along, and by the time they had descended upon them, they had disappeared entirely. Jack stood up. "Shall we?" he asked, holding a hand out. "Sure," Diane said, taking it. And together they went, hand in hand, for one last stroll through the rooms, the museum, the garden, the horse field, the courtyard, the pool, the theatre, and everything else that comprised the tiny, self-contained little paradise that they had created out of their own minds. And then they watched as it disappeared completely.

And there they were, back on the curb in front of the amusement park, with Attalos standing before them, a broad smile on his face, which was now that of a human, not a lizard. On the ground, all around them, were the men who had attacked them, laying there frozen in place. "Congratulations," Attalos said, "You made it through the third city—The land of the tempting reptile. Job well done."

"*You* were our guide?" Diane asked, confused. "He gave me a few helpful hints," Jack explained. Then he furrowed his brow and added with a sneer, "But he could have made it a *lot* easier."

"I wasn't there to make it easier my friend," Attalos smiled. "Just to help you through."

"Yeah," Jack said. "You wouldn't happen to know what the next city might be, would you?"

"Well . . ." Attalos said, "I'm really not supposed to say."

"Come on, if you know, tell us."

"Very well. Your next city is Sheol. Land of the dead."

"Sounds delightful," Jack said.

Attalos ignored the sarcasm and said simply, "Good luck to you on the rest of your journey." And then, looking down at the attackers, he added "You might want to get a move on. They will not remain frozen for long."

"Lovely," Jack said. They said their good byes and made their way back to the car. Smokey was in the back, exactly as they had left him. Diane started the car up and within minutes they were back on route 44, headed toward Oklahoma.

18

THEY DROVE IN SILENCE for almost an hour. Jack didn't know why they didn't speak. Perhaps there was nothing to say; perhaps there was *too much* to say, and neither knew where to begin. Jack believed it was the latter. They were like two ships being tossed by the waves, in every direction, with no end in sight. And they had just exchanged a lifetime of guaranteed peace and prosperity in exchange for the continued hazards, travails, and terrors of their current course. Jack felt a sadness about the whole thing, deepened by a sense that however the journey ended, it wouldn't matter. "Penny for your thoughts," Diane said.

"You don't want to hear my thoughts," Jack said.

"Sure, I do," Diane replied, "Or I wouldn't have asked."

"I just think this mission is a waste of time."

"How so?"

"Well, think about it. What are we trying to do? Show people the way back to the garden of Eden, right?"

"Uh huh."

"Well, think about it. Since when do people want to be shown the error of their ways? You think we're the first ones to try it? Anytime someone comes with a message like that, you know what people do? They kill them. Anyone who comes to people with a message of peace, a message of hope, a message of love; they kill them. John Kennedy came with that message. They killed him. Robert Kennedy came with that message. They killed him. John Lennon came with that message. They killed him. Mahatma Gandhi came with that message. They killed him. Martin Luther King came with that message. They killed him. Jesus Christ came with that message. They killed him. So, why should we be any different? People don't want to change.

They don't want to think for themselves. And they don't want to love each other. And nobody's ever going to change that."

"You might be right, Jack," Diane said. "I don't know. But I didn't accept this mission because I wanted to change the world."

"Then why did you?"

"Because I was called."

"Yeah," Jack said, "Called." And then he was quiet. So was she, for the next twenty minutes. Then Jack's cell phone rang. It was his mother. He spoke for several minutes. Toward the end of the conversation, he took a pen and piece of paper out of the glove compartment and jotted down an address. Then he hung up. He stared straight ahead, saying nothing, as a knot twisted its way through his stomach, like a big fist was inside of him, clenching his guts. Diane put a hand on his lap. "I'm sorry," she said. She had heard enough of the conversation to get the gist: his father was dying in a hospice somewhere; he had written the address on that paper. "Where is he?" she asked. "Tulsa," Jack replied. "That's not that far from here," she said. "We can be there in less than three hours."

"This is the address," he said, handing her the paper. She handed it back to him and said, "Okay, we're on our way."

A few hundred miles later they were in Tulsa. As they were driving through midtown, Jack said out of the blue, "Let me drive; I want to go visit my mother." They switched seats and Jack started driving. "When is the last time you saw her?" Diane asked. "Two years ago, when I ran away."

"It's a risk to go there, you know," Diane said. "I know," Jack responded. "But I want to see her."

"I understand," Diane said.

Jack weaved through a few side streets, and within minutes, pulled into the driveway of his mom's home. As they got out, Jack grabbed Smokey from the back, saying, "My mother's a cat person."

"Does she have any?" Diane asked.

"Two: Schnuckims and Pookey." Jack put the cat down on the porch and rang the bell. A few minutes later his mother answered. She was wearing jeans and a T shirt. Jack was surprised at how much weight she had lost, but otherwise she looked good. She had always been an attractive woman, with thin features, bright green eyes, and lustrous auburn hair that spilled onto her shoulders. She waited for them to get in, then threw her arms around her son, crying, "Oh Adam, you've lost so much weight!"

"You too," he smiled, grabbing her by the shoulders and taking a good look at her. She laughed, and they hugged again. Then she looked at Diane and said, "And this must be the one you told me about!" Diane smiled awkwardly. "It's a pleasure to meet you Mrs. Horn," Diane said, extending a hand. "Call me Sara," she said, ignoring the hand and giving Diane a big hug. "Okay, I will," Diane gasped, amazed at the strength of this this small, slender woman. "So, how has my son been treating you?" Sara demanded. "Well, he's a bit of a crank," Diane said, "but other than that, I have no complaints." Sara laughed. She had a big, pearly white smile, like those woman in the toothpaste commercials. "And who is this?" she asked, scooping up Smokey in her arms, and stroking it behind the ears, causing it to purr gratefully. Clearly, she had a way with cats. "This is Smokey," Jack said. "He kind of adopted me when I was sleeping in the park."

"Until I adopted *him* and gave him a real bed," Diane interjected. They all laughed at that. "Well, she's a beauty," Sara said, calling out "Schnuckims, Pookey; we have visitors." The two cats came hurrying out of the kitchen as Sara put Smokey down. The three felines quickly fell into a scrummage of sniffing, pawing, and playing. "Come and sit down," Sara said, pointing to the dining room table, which had been set with three place settings. "I've been cooking for three hours."

"Wait a second," Jack said. "I didn't tell you I was coming here. How did you know?"

"I just know," she said, "I *am* your mother. Now sit." They obeyed as she disappeared into the kitchen. Diane smiled at Jack and whispered, "I love her."

"Yeah, well you haven't been around her that long yet," Jack answered. Moments later Sara came out with a large platter of roasted beef, garnished with peas, and placed it on the table. She made three more trips to the kitchen, bringing out, in succession: buttered biscuits, cranberry sauce, corn, carrots, apple sauce, and two kinds of soda—Coke and Orange. "Hope you guys are hungry," she said, as she finally took her seat. "Starving," Diane said. "I'll second that," Jack said, grabbing a large knife and carving the beef into thin slices, which he distributed to his mother, Diane, and then himself. As they dug into the feast, the cats crept up to the table in pursuit of scraps. "Oh, I haven't forgotten about you guys," Sarah said. Then she got up and led them into the kitchen, where three bowls of cat food were waiting. Upon returning she said, "That should keep them out of our hair for a while." Then she added, "I don't know what I'd do without my kitties. The house has been so lonely since Adam left."

A sad, awkward silence ensued, as they all knew it was about to get a lot lonelier with her husband at death's door. Indeed, he was already gone, in a sense, living out his remaining days in a hospice. But Sara didn't want to go there just yet; she hadn't seen her son in two years and she wanted to enjoy him for a little while. A little while was all she had, as Jack planned to move on. One visit to the hospice, and then they would hit the road. But that was something they did not discuss just yet. Instead they talked about just about everything else, including the mission. Sara wanted to know all about it. Where did they go? What did they do? How long would it last? How would they know when it was finished? Why had they been chosen? They answered the questions as best they could. She seemed utterly amazed by everything they said, even as she was frightened by the obvious danger involved. When the meal was finished, they moved the party to the living area, where they had coffee and pastry. Diane and his mom sat on the sofa, while Jack sat on the love seat perpendicular to them. In between them was a lamp on a small table; on the floor was a coffee table and an area rug with an image of a nature scene woven into it. After a short round of small talk, Sara said, "I want the two of you to stay here for a while."

"We can't, mom; it's not safe. Every minute we stay here we put you at risk." She leaned over and clasped his hand. "Listen to me," she said, staring intently into his eyes. "Two years ago, I lost you. Now I am losing Peter. I want to spend some time with my son. If it gets me killed, so be it. I don't care. Will you stay with me for a while?" Jack stared helplessly at Diane, who nodded her assent. Then he stared back at his mother, sighed, and said "Okay. We'll stay."

"Great!" she said. "The two of you can stay in your old room. I will make it up."

"That's fine," Jack said.

"I'm so glad to see you again, Adam," she said, with tears in her eyes, and gave him another hug. "I love you, mom," he said. When they were finished with their coffee, Jack said, "I think I ought to go see dad now."

"Yes, why don't we all go?" Sara suggested.

"Okay," Jack said, and the three of them left for the hospice.

∽

The hospice was a short drive from Sarah's home. They parked in the lot and filed in, through the front door, up to the front desk. A woman in a pink uniform, wearing a bonnet on her head, signed them in and started giving them directions. "Thank you, I know where it is," Sara said. She led them down a long, carpeted hallway to a room on the right. Room 104. "This is his room," she said. "Why don't I go in first and prepare him. Seeing you after all these years will be quite a shock."

"Sure," Jack said. He and Diane waited outside, on a bench by a window at the end of the hallway. After a short while, she came out, a kind of sad, small smile on her face, and said "Okay. You can go in now." Jack clasped Diane's hand, took a deep breath, and approached room 104 to see his father for the first time in two years. He paused at the doorway for a moment, looking down at his shoes, then strolled in. He had braced himself for the worst, but it was even worse than he had imagined. His father lay there, propped up in bed with an IV in one arm and a thin blanket covering him up to his chest. He was pale and emaciated. Worse of all, his eyes looked bloodshot and weak. The spark that had always been there was gone, as if he had died already and was just waiting to be buried.

Jack approached him and stood by the side of the bed. "Hi, dad," he said. "Hello Adam," his father replied. Jack really didn't know what to say. What do you say to someone whose dying, and who you haven't spoken to for two years. Do you talk about the weather? Sports? Current events? Jack didn't know. Fortunately, his father broke the silence, saying "How have you been?"

"Not too bad," Jack said. He didn't really know if that was the truth or not. His father pointed to a chair by the window. "Sit down," he said. Jack pulled the seat up and sat down. "You travel around a lot these days," his father said. "Yes," Jack replied, "Not by choice, though."

"They still want to kill you," Peter said. "They are agents of Satan." Jack did not think his enemy was Satan; he believed it was the church. But he couldn't tell his father that—a man who spent his whole life in the church. "Yes," Jack said simply. He really didn't want to discuss the mission with his father at all. Peter had felt the mission was something sacred and had been appalled when his son did not share his enthusiasm for it. He wanted to be a part of it; he felt it was *their* calling, *their* mission, not just Jack's. Jack's attitude toward the mission drove a wedge between the two, and when he ran away and refused to even talk to his father about it—or anything else—for two years, that wedge grew even deeper.

Jack decided to change the subject. "Mom is looking well," he said. "Your mother is a strong woman," Peter said. "She has had to endure a lot. She lost a lot of weight since you ran away." *Was driven away* Jack wanted to say, but he didn't. He could tell his father was spoiling for a fight and he didn't want to give it to him. Again, he changed the subject. "I have met someone," he said. His father just gave him a blank stare and said, "A girl, I hope."

"Yes, a girl," Jack said. "How'd you meet her?" Peter asked, his tone softening a little bit. "At a job." Peter nodded his head approvingly. "Good. Better than meeting someone in a bar. Is it serious?"

"Very," Jack said.

"I would like to meet this young lady sometime," Peter said. Jack hesitated for a second, then said "Well, you can meet her right now if you like."

"Bring her in," Peter said.

Jack went back out into the hall, where his mother and Diane were sitting together, and said to Diane "Dad would like to meet you, if that's okay."

"Of course," Diane said, getting up. Sara smiled at the two of them as they headed toward the room.

"This is Diane," Jack said, as the two of them approached his bed. Upon seeing her Peter's eyes, so dead just moments before, lit up like the lights on a Christmas tree. "Well, Jack," he said with a grin, "Looks like you finally did something right. She's beautiful." Then he extended his hand and said, "Nice to meet you, darling."

"It's my pleasure," Diane said, shaking his hand. "So, tell me," Peter said, "What is it you saw in this guy, anyway?"

"Well," she said, sidling up to Jack and talking his arm in her hands, "He's handsome. He's smart. He's funny. Did I leave anything out, Jack?"

"Charming and fearless," Jack replied with a grin.

"You sure we're talking about the same person?" Peter asked.

"I'm positive," Diane said.

"If you insist," Peter replied.

A kind of awkward silence ensued, which Peter broke by saying "Well, maybe you two can come and see me again sometime."

"I'd like that very much," Diane said. "See you tomorrow, dad," Jack said, and led Diane out of the room, back to his mother, who stood up as they approached. "Well," Jack said, "After twenty-two years, me and dad finally found something we could agree on." The three laughed as they headed back to the car.

The next day they went back. Once again Sarah went in first, then Jack followed. He found his father as he had left him, propped up in bed, with an IV in one arm, looking pale and emaciated. But there was a bit more life in his eyes today, and Jack thought that might have something to do with his visit. "Where's the girl?" his father said immediately, apparently more interested in seeing her than in seeing him. For that Jack really couldn't blame him. "She's out in the hall with mom; I thought maybe we could talk a little first."

"You really lucked out with her," Peter said. "You're right about that," Jack agreed. Never one for small talk, Peter said "So tell me about this mission of yours. When does it start?"

"It already started," Jack said, although he had no intention of recounting the exact details; his father might think he was insane, and besides, he didn't really want to relive all of that horror. He just filled him in on the basics, giving him a kind of abbreviated version of the events of the last few days. "Sounds like some kind of LSD trip," Peter said. "Yeah," Jack replied, "Well, that's what it feels like."

"So, how's this supposed to help humanity? Isn't that your mission? To show the world the way back to the garden of Eden?"

"Well, the mission's not over yet," Jack said, wishing he had not divulged any of this to his father. "Not over?" Peter growled, "Well, how many tree people and talking snakes do you have to wrestle with before it's over? And how's any of that gonna help anybody?"

"Look, dad, I know you're upset about not being part of this mission, but I . . ."

Peter laughed. "Upset? About not getting to run around with you on your little drug trips?"

"They weren't drug trips," Jack said, his anger rising.

"So, what have you learned?" he sneered, his voice full of contempt. "You went through all of these mystical journeys of discovery; so, what have you actually learned?"

"Maybe this was a bad idea," Jack said, and turned to leave.

"Maybe choosing *you* for this mission was a bad idea. God should have picked someone with half a brain, who could actually learn something."

That was it; Jack had had enough. "You want to know what I learned?" he snarled, "I'll tell you! I learned there was no Eden. It's just another fairy tale the church tells us. I learned the garden wasn't some magical place that two perfect people got kicked out of. *We* are the garden and the tree in the middle is our nervous system and the tempting reptile is our brain and when we were kicked out of the garden we were kicked out of ourselves!" He paused to catch his breath. He was on a roll now and it felt good. He continued: "I learned a little about John 15:6: "If a man abide not in me, he is cast forth as a branch, and is withered; and men gather them, and cast them into the fire, and they are burned." He was not talking about throwing real people into a real fire; he was talking about our *thoughts*. Any thought not rooted in truth will be destroyed by fire; like it says in 1 Corinthians 3:15: "If any man's work shall be burned, he shall suffer loss; but he himself shall be saved, yet so as fire."

And I learned God doesn't like guilt. He doesn't want us carrying around that weight of guilt and regret and tormenting ourselves with it and tormenting each *other* with it like preachers do from the pulpit."

Jack stopped there. He had made his point. Peter just stared at him, his face blank, and said "Guess you learned a thing or two after all," he said. "Sounds like you learned that everything I believe is a lie, is that it? Everything I ever learned, everything I ever taught, everything I ever preached; it was all a lie? Is that what you learned? That my whole life was a lie?"

Peter was getting excited now, too excited for a man in his condition, and Jack decided it was time to go. His father kept shouting as he left. As Jack turned out of his father's room and started back, he heard a whistle coming from room 106, the one right next to his father's. He stopped and looked in. An old man waved him in. He went in. He was greeted by an old black man, gaunt and haggard, with a scraggly grey beard and oxygen tubes in his nose. He was sitting in a deep arm chair; next to the chair was an oxygen tank; opposite the chair was his bed and a window. He was wearing a pair of loose fitting brown pants and a flannel shirt; around his shoulders was a thin, yellow blanket.

"Come here, son," the man said, "Sit down." Jack sat on the edge of the bed, facing the old man, who he figured to be in his eighties. "My name is Grady," the man said, extending his hand. "Pleased to meet you," Jack said, shaking the man's hand. "These walls are kind of thin," Grady said, pointing to the wall behind him with his thumb. "I couldn't help overhearing."

"Sorry about that," Jack said, "I didn't mean to get so loud."

"That's okay," Grady smiled, "I had a father, too, and I used to fight with him, too—about some of the same stuff you were just fighting about in there."

"Really?" Jack said.

"Oh, yeah," the man said. "We fought all the time. *All* the time. You see, my parents were very religious, too, and me . . . well, I wasn't."

"Was your father a preacher, too?" Jack asked.

"No, he wasn't a preacher," Grady said, shaking his head, "But that didn't stop him from preaching!" He threw his head back and laughed. Jack laughed, too. "Here's the thing," Brady said, "We all got the same problem. That problem is death. Whether you're a young man, like you, with lots of years left, or an old man like me, with just a few months, we are all dying. And when people are faced with dying, they panic. It's like a drowning man. He reaches out for anything he could find to keep him afloat. A piece of driftwood, an inner tube, a raft . . . Whatever's there, he'll try and grab it. Well, that's how it is with people and dying. We reach for whatever's nearest. If you're Catholic, you reach for the priest and the sacraments. If you're Protestant, you reach for the Pastor and the sinner's prayer. If you're a Muslim, you reach for the Koran and a prayer rug. And what do you get when you reach for those things? Well, you get the whole package. A whole system of beliefs, doctrines, dogmas, rituals. And you adopt those beliefs. Those doctrines. Those dogmas. Those rituals. And you're assured, by the people in that system, that you have found the one, true way to get to heaven and escape hell. So, you cling to that . . ." The man made a grabbing gesture with his hands. "like a drowning man grabbing an inner tube. And you hold on for dear life. 'Because you've found your way out. Your way out of death. And anything or anyone that comes along that challenges that, you push it away, instinctively, without even thinking, because it threatens your very life, your very *soul*. And so that thing you grabbed onto to, to escape death; that thing becomes your God, and you become its slave. That very thing you're clinging to for *life* becomes *death*, but you don't even know it. You *can't* know it, cause now, you're on the *inside*, and you can't see it clearly from the inside. All of these systems, from the *outside* we can see how crazy they are. The Protestants can see how crazy the Catholics are; the Catholics can see how crazy the Muslims are; the Muslims can see how crazy the Jehovahs are; the Jehovah's can see how crazy the Mormons are; but no-one can see how crazy their *own* system is cause they're on the *inside*. You see what I mean?"

"Yes, I see," Jack said. And he did. Clearly.

"So, take it easy on your old man," Grady said, tapping him on the knee. "He's just a drowning man, clinging to what he knows best. And you upset him today. You pulled the rug out from him; took away that inner tube just when he needed it most. Now . . . he has to face death without his *system* of beliefs to protect him. And that's a scary thing."

"I guess I should have kept my mouth shut," Jack said.

"Oh no," Grady said, "You just gotta go back and make it right."

"But how do I do that?"

"Son," the man said, looking at him intently, "You underestimate yourself. I heard you speaking in there. You *will* make it right. But maybe not today. He's all worked up now. Come back tomorrow and try again."

And with that the man leaned back in his chair and took several deep breaths. "I'm sorry, son," he said. "That's all the talking I can do for now. But you come see me tomorrow after you talk to your dad again and tell me how it turned out."

Jack thanked the man and left, heading back down the hall to his mom and Diane.

⌒

When Jack went home, he did something he had not done for a long time. He read his bible, with Grady's words still fresh in his mind: *You gotta make it right.* He wanted to do that. He wanted to make things right. He didn't want to disappoint the old man; he didn't want to disappoint himself; and, most of all, he didn't want to disappoint his father.

But he knew there was only one language his dad understood—the language of scripture. So, he set out to find from that scripture something that would show his father that he *had* been wrong about God, and that he ought to be *glad* he was wrong about him. The pursuit kept him up until five in the morning, but when he was done, he thought he had accomplished what he had set out to accomplish. He would find out later that day.

⌒

Peter was looking better when Jack entered the room. He was not in bed; he was sitting in a chair by the window. There was no IV in his arm. Jack suspected that his visits, as tense as they were, had sparked some life back into the old man's bones. There was another chair in the room. Jack grabbed it, placed it opposite his father, and sat down. There the two of them sat, facing each other, as if in a standoff. "How are you feeling today?" Jack asked. "As well as can be expected," Peter answered, his voice betraying no emotion. If he was angry about yesterday, it was not apparent. For a moment Jack thought about letting the whole thing ride; just make some small talk and forget about it, but he couldn't do that. He had to *make it right.*

"So, did you have good talk with Grady, yesterday?" Peter asked.

"Yes, actually, I did."

"What'd he say?"

"He said not to be so hard on you. He said that when people are facing death, they need control. And they find it in their theological systems."

"Is that so?"

"Yes."

"And you think that's what I have done?"

"Yes, and I can prove it."

"And how's that?" Peter challenged.

"How do you interpret the bible?"

"I use the bible. I compare scripture with scripture."

"So, if a verse deals with a particular subject, you cannot truly know the meaning of that verse, for certain, until you have read every other verse that pertains to that subject?"

"I suppose you could put it that way."

"Is there another way to put it?"

"Okay, I will put it that way. Fine."

"Okay, lets test that. Let's say the subject is the atonement. Let's designate the atonement by use of the letter A. Every verse that deals with the Atonement is A. Let's say there are 50 such verses. We have A1 through A50. Okay?"

"Sure."

"So, you're reading your bible. You come to the first verse that pertains to the atonement. Let's call it verse A1. It presents the Atonement in a certain light. Now, say you get to A2, and it casts a slightly *different* light on the Atonement. Do you interpret A1 in light of A2? Or A2 in light of A1? Or do we suspend any judgment at all until we read verses A3 through A50, some of which will agree with A1, some which will agree with A2, and some which will cast a different, third or fourth of fifth light on the atonement? And how is it even possible to read words without attaching meaning to them? Suspending all judgment, making our minds a blank, until we have read all fifty verses? When you say this is how you interpret your bible, you are implying that you have this ability. Do you?"

"I suppose no-one does."

"Exactly! Then the bible cannot be interpreted that way. And if we do we will always end up with what we have now: schism. A vast multiplicity of different interpretations, all that have substantial scriptural support."

"Then how do we interpret the bible?"

"By the spirit. The bible says the letter kills, but the spirit gives life. And that, dad, is what my mission is about. I am learning the spiritual meaning of the scriptures, truths that we have killed by our obsession with the letter."

Peter said nothing. He just said there, a pensive expression on his face. To his surprise, Jack actually thought he was getting through. He decided to press his advantage. "Listen to me; your interpretation of the bible, by the letter, has led you to believe that God tortures most people in hell forever, right?"

"Yes, it has."

"Well, what if I can give you another interpretation, by the letter, that would seem to suggest that God has promised to save everyone?"

"I'm listening."

"Okay, well then listen to these three verses of scripture." Jack read the three verses: first, Philippians 2:9-11:"he was given a name which is above every name, that at the name of Jesus every knee should bow, of things in heaven, and things in earth, and things under the earth; and that every tongue should confess that Jesus Christ is Lord, to the glory of God the Father."

Then, Romans 10:9: "if we confess with the mouth the Lord Jesus and believe in the heart that God hath raised him from the dead, we shall be saved."

Then, 1 Corinthians 12:3: "No-one can say that Jesus is Lord, except by the Holy Ghost."

Then he said, "Now, these three verses, taken together, in their natural context, seem to teach, without question, that God will save everyone who ever lived, right?"

"Yes, I suppose they do?"

There were a lot things Jack could have said after that, but he felt he had made his point. He just sat there and waited for his father to speak. For a long time, he didn't; he just sat there, staring into space. Then he said "Son, I think maybe they picked the right guy for this mission, after all."

Jack smiled as the two men embraced, *really* embraced, for the first time in their lives.

On the way out, Jack stopped in to see Grady, who he found in the same chair, in the same position, as the previous day. "So, how'd it go?" he asked. Jack answered with a thumbs up sign. Grady returned it and said, "Good man."

"So," Jack asked, "What's your last name?" He remembered the previous guides: Brady, Taylor, Attalos: none of them had two names. "It's just Grady," the man smiled. "That's what I thought," Jack said. He recalled what the previous guide, Attalos, had said. The next city would be Sheol, land of the dead. His research, though, had told him that wasn't entirely correct. Sheol was the land where the dead were still alive, existing in a condition somewhere between the two states. It was the land of the *living* dead, which perfectly described his father's condition. On that note, Jack left, happy that he had made peace with his father, and wondering what came next. It didn't take much to realize that Grady had been his guide for this fourth city, and that in helping his father pass from death to life, he had completed the task assigned. "So, I guess I made it through Sheol," Jack said. "I guess you did," Grady said with a smile.

19

THE NEXT THOUSAND MILES passed without incident, as they headed into the Utah desert. They had stayed for three full days at Jack's mother's, then decided it was time to move on. Sara was sad, but she understood. Now they were only about five hundred miles away from Disneyland, and three cities away from completing their mission. They weren't sure which destination they would reach first.

As they were driving down a mostly abandoned stretch of highway, a middle-aged woman came running toward them, waving her arms wildly, her boobs jiggling in her sweat soaked blouse. She was wearing a pair of short pants and had no shoes on. She had thick, shoulder length black hair and appeared to be of Hispanic descent. As she ran toward them she was yelling "Help me, Help me."

They stopped and got out of the car. She ran right up to them, still screaming. "Calm down, calm down!" Jack said, grabbing her by the shoulders. "Help me, they'll kill me! They'll kill me!" the woman shouted.

Diane got into the back seat with her and Jack kept driving. "Oh, thank you, thank you," she said, in a thick accent, and then again started up with "They'll kill me, they'll kill me."

"Please, mam, try to calm down. Who? Who is trying to kill you?"

"My slave masters. I escaped. They will kill me when they catch me."

"Slave masters?" Diane repeated.

"Oh yes, they are terrible. They make us work night and day, no rest, no food, nothing. I couldn't take it anymore. I had to get out!"

"Well, listen," Diane said, "You're safe with us. We won't let anything happen to you."

"Oh, thank you. God bless you."

"Who is keeping you as a slave?" Jack asked, wondering if this woman might be on a bad acid trip, psychotic, or just confused. "The nephilim," she said. "They rule the town. They make us work night and day; they pay us a few cents and keep everything for themselves. They live like kings and queens while we live like animals!"

"The nephilim?" Diane asked. She was familiar with the term. It was from Genesis 6:4, and it described a race of half humans/half Gods that supposedly existed in ancient times. Most scholars did not think there was any truth to it. "Yes, the nephilim!" the woman said. "Oh, they are terrible! They are monsters!"

As she was speaking a number of large, all-terrain vehicles were approaching them—thick, steel structures that looked like something that belonged on a battlefield rather than the roads. They were not on the highway; they were coming at them from the empty stretch of grassland on the side. "It's them!" the woman shouted, "They've found me. Oh, no! Oh, no!"

The vehicles surrounded the car, forcing Jack to stop. Then the occupants of the vehicles got out and approached. They were terrible indeed—massive men, built like rocks, with gigantic chests, bulging biceps, and huge hands; they had sharp, angular features, and wore dark glasses strapped around their small, sloping, shaven heads. They wore big boots that were tucked into their pants. They looked on average about seven feet tall and Jack guessed that they probably possessed the strength of gorillas.

Jack locked all the doors and went for the glock in his backpack. As he reached for it a hand crashed through the window and punched him in the head. Then the same hand opened the door, yanked him out, and dragged him toward one of the vehicles. Within seconds all three of them had been removed from the car and placed in the backseats of the huge, ugly vehicles; Jack in one and Diane and the woman in another. With their prisoners safely in tow, the creatures took off.

Jack watched out the window as they rolled through the desert, through back roads, swamps, over bridges, and finally, down a narrow dirt path that led to a town named San Milo, according to the sign just before its entrance. As they drove through the town, Jack did not notice anything particularly conspicuous. It seemed like an ordinary place, except that it was populated entirely by two classes of people: the nephilim and the slaves. As they drove along, he saw plenty of both. The nephilim walked about freely; the slaves were always busy doing some kind of job, usually with one or more nephilim nearby, supervising. The tasks were menial in nature: picking weeds, working in a field, mowing lawns, and so on. One of them was kneeling over a flower bed, digging into the soil, with a nephilim standing over him with a boot on his back. Jack found himself filling with anger at the sight.

A short time later the two vehicles arrived at a small, official looking building, with a flag flying from its roof. The nephilim dragged them out of the cars and took them into the building. Inside there were two rows of desks, with two in each row, with filing cabinets off to the side, and a printer against the back wall. Only one of the desks was occupied. On that desk was a large name plate that read *Slave master*, and sitting there a nephilim, who was even bigger and more fierce looking than the others. Upon seeing the escaped prisoner, he stood up and approached. He wore a gray uniform, with a badge on his chest, and a hat on his head. He looked at the woman, staring her up and down, then broke into a wide grin. His teeth were very large, filling his whole mouth, and they appeared to be made of iron. Everything about him—everything about all of the nephilim—was big and cruel and menacing, as if they had been designed in a laboratory by a mad scientist seeking to create the most frightening specimen possible. "Who are they?" he asked in a voice that sounded like a creaking door. "They were helping her escape," one of the nephilim said. "Take them out back," the slave master said.

Out back was a yard, surrounded by trees. In the middle was a very low, smooth tree stump with an axe lying across it. The slave master picked up the axe, and said, "Put her leg on it." Then, looking at Jack and Diane, he said "This is what we do to slaves who try to escape."

The woman screamed horribly as they stretched her leg over the stump. Without a moment's hesitation, the slave master raised the axe, then brought it down on the woman's leg, just below the knee, slicing it clean off. As the women screamed in agony, one of the nephilim hoisted her over his shoulders like a rag doll and carried her off, presumably to a hospital. "It is not good to try to escape," the slave master said, the axe perched on his shoulder. Then he whistled and called out "Spike!" Moments later a massive dog came running along, it's tongue dripping with sweat, and started sniffing at the bloody stump of leg on the tree stump. Then it started eating it, gulping down huge chucks of flesh, until there was almost nothing left. Then it belched and ran off. "Atta boy," the slave master said, then cut his eyes first to Jack and Diane, then to the other two Nephilim. "Take them to their quarters," he said. "The midtown barracks."

"Yes sir," they said as one and brought them back around the side of the buildings, to their vehicles. One of them got in the back seat with Jack and Diane while the other drove. Within minutes they had arrived at the barracks—a sprawling, one level edifice surrounded by a chain link fence.

They were led into the building, down a hallway. As they walked along, one of the nephilim said "I'll take her; you take him." They were led into small rooms, across the hall from each other. Jack looked around the room. It had a scale, a blood pressure cuff, and a locker. On the wall by the door was a phone. The nephilim dialed an extension on the phone and said, with his door creaking voice "Mayla, please come into the initiation office; we have two new ones." Moments later a female nephilim in a nurse uniform entered the room, a clipboard in her hand. She ordered Jack to stand against the wall while she asked some questions. Name, age, birth date, place of residence, etc . . . Then she took his weight and blood pressure, marking the results on her file. When she was done, she said simply "Okay, he appears to be in good health; you can place him in with the general population" and left.

The nephilim grabbed some cloths out of a locker and tossed them at Jack, saying "Put them on." Jack looked at them. It was a uniform, dull brown, made of a thin polyester fabric, like the ones prisoners wear. Jack though about throwing it right back into the nephilim's face, but then thought better of it. These cats didn't mess around; he saw what they did to the woman. Better to play along, bide his time, and wait for a chance to escape. He put the uniform on.

"Come on," the nephilim said, leading him down a long hallway, and into a large barracks, filled with slaves. Each slave, it appeared, shared a small space with another; in that space was a bunk bed and two dressers. Along the sides of the barracks were some chairs and sofas, by the windows. The nephilim approached an older man who was lying on his bed and said, "This is Jack. He's new. Find him a spot."

"He can stay with me, Mr. Copeland," the man said. "My old roommate died last week."

"Good," Copeland said, "You show him the ropes." Then he turned and left. "Hi, my name is Sawyer," the man said, extending a hand. He was an older man, with a thin mustache, an even thinner frame, and a kind, gentle way about him that Jack liked. Jack shook his hand and said, "Hello; nice to meet you." That was a lie, of course. It was not nice to meet him. Meeting this man, and being in this place, was not nice at all.

"These guys don't fool around, do they?" Jack said. A serious, almost grave expression crept onto the man's face as he said, "No, they don't." It sounded like a warning, and Sawyer just stared at him for a few moments, as if to say *You got that, sonny?* Then he said, "Come on, I'll show you around."

The barracks was laid out in a very simple fashion. A thin lane ran down the middle; on the sides, near the windows, were some benches and chairs, where the slaves could relax. And off to the left, down a hall, were communal showers and bathrooms. The women were housed in an identical barracks on the other side of the building where, he presumed, Diane was currently being confined. In another building, behind that one, was a mess hall, where they were served three meals a day.

When they got back to their quarters, Jack asked, "So, how long have you been in this place?"

"All my life," Sawyer replied, sitting down on his bunk. Jack sat next to him. "I thought slavery was illegal," Jack said. "Well, if it is, that's news to me," Sawyer said. Jack stared at him, dumfounded. How could this man, who was not stupid, not know that slavery was illegal? Jack decided not to press the issue. "So, what do they make you do?" he asked.

"Little bit of everything," Sawyer replied.

"Like what?"

Sawyer shrugged. "Whatever needs doing. We till the fields; we mow lawns; pick weeds; walk dogs; we work in the factories, the warehouses, the plants; we do whatever they don't want to do themselves."

"I see," Jack said. "What do they have *you* doing?"

"Last few months I been working on the Powers Plantation, cutting tobacco stalks. That's right here in midtown; probably where they'll put you, too."

"What about families?"

"What about them?"

"Do slaves have families? Do they get married, have children?"

"Oh no, how can we do that? Men and women live in separate quarters. Only time we see each other is out in the fields, picking cotton or tobacco or something like that."

"So, you can never have families?"

"Well, some of the women have kids. But I wouldn't call it a family."

"What do you mean?"

STEPHEN CAMPANA

"Well, sometimes the nephilim have relations with the slave women and they have children. But the children grow up in orphanages, raised by slaves."

"That's terrible," Jack said. "How can you . . ."

"Shhhh!" Sawyer said, looking around nervously. "The other slaves will hear you."

"So what?" Jack said in a lower voice.

"They'll tell," Sawyer snarled, his voice filled with anger and frustration. "Why do you ask all these questions? Where are you from?"

"I'm from the outside," Jack said. "I was just taken here today."

"Well, that explains it," Sawyer said. "You do not know how things world around here. I will tell you more, but not right now. I don't want to talk no more," he said.

And for the rest of the day, they didn't.

⤳

The next day, at dawn, Jack was shaken violently from sleep. He woke with a start to the grim face of Mr. Copeland, standing there at the foot of his upper bunk. His eyes were level with Copeland's, staring right into the lens of those tinted black glasses. "Get up!" he said; "You'll be out in the Powers plantation today. Get dressed and get outside."

He did. When he got outside, there were two buses waiting. He and about four dozen other prisoners, male and female, got onto the buses, with a little help from two nephilims, who herded them like sheep, before boarding the buses themselves. The buses traveled, one behind the other, to the Powers plantation—a massive swath of land, filled with tobacco stalks, that sprawled out in all directions as far as the eye could see. About a hundred yards in the distance was the Powers mansion. Next to it was a silo of some kind, and in the driveway a number of expensive looking cars. As they filed out of the bus, they were handed sickles and sent out into the field to begin work. As they walked through the stalks, Jack saw Diane. She looked back at him and the two nodded. He didn't dare go over to her just yet; it would look too conspicuous, and he was afraid the nephilim might take that as a cue to keep them separated. It would better to bide his time.

And it was a *lot* of time. All day, from sun up to sun down, he cut the stalks. It wasn't so bad for the first six hours, when it was relatively cool, but the next six were pure murder, as the temperature climbed slowly to almost a hundred degrees. They were permitted only brief breaks, every few hours, to drink water or eat something. If they had to go to the bathroom, they had to use one of the several port a potties that had been set up along the sides of the plantation. There was no shade; nothing at all to protect them. All day long the sun beat down on them like a drum. Several times people feinted. When this happened a nephilim would carry them over to the sides, splash some water on them, and wait for them to wake up. Then they would send them right back out into the field. It was like nothing Jack had ever witnessed, a cruelty beyond imagining.

Around midday he and Diane made their way over to one another, and, while working, exchanged some words. She was learning all she could and working on a way out; that was about all she could say at that point, and Jack had little to add. All they could do for now was bide their time and try to stay alive.

When the work day was over, at about six o'clock, they all filed back into the buses, which took them back to the barracks. Soaked with sweat, and barely able to stand, they filed into the barracks, and headed straight for the showers. Jack could not recall a shower ever feeling so good. He was exhausted; every muscle in his body ached. He was not used to this kind of work and there was no initiation period; they just tossed you in and that was it.

After the showers the slaves went to the mess hall—a large cafeteria with rows of tables. Plates in hand the slaves got in line for their food, which was served by other slaves from behind a counter. They took the plates to the tables and ate. When they were finished, they went back to the barracks. It was all very precise and efficient; no fuss, no muss. No-one complained; no-one got hurt. This was just another day in the life of a slave in San Milo.

That evening, as Jack and Sawyer sat together in their cubicle, Jack said, "So, tell me about these nephilim." He had heard about them from the bible; supposedly they were a race of people that were created when angels mated with humans. But he wanted Sawyer's take on it. "Well, they are Gods," he said.

"Who told you that?" Jack asked.

"They did."

"They told you?" Jack said. "How do you know they are telling the truth?"

"They show us from the bible. It says it right in there. Genesis 6:4."

"And do you read the bible?"

"Most slaves cannot read. But a few can read a little. They will tell you; it's right there in the bible. The nephilim are what they say they are. And besides, if they weren't, how could they have all that power?"

"Why don't they teach you to read?"

"Because for the things we do, we don't have to read."

"Maybe if you could read, you could do better things."

"Maybe," Sawyer shrugged, "But who are we to question the nephilim? Besides, they read the bible to us. In the temples."

"They let you go to their temples?"

"Of course."

"You actually pray with these . . . things?"

"We pray *to* them," Sawyer said.

"*To* them?" Jack repeated.

"Of course. Remember, they are the children of God! We are just the children of men."

"But Jesus said, 'Do you not know you are Gods' And he said that to *men*."

"I have never heard about that verse," Sawyer said.

"Of course not," Jack said.

"I don't think we should talk about this anymore," Sawyer said, his voice filling with same anger he had yesterday.

"Suit yourself," Jack shrugged.

For the rest of the night they talked only about less consequential matters, then turned in around eight o'clock. Jack was exhausted, and he slept well.

The next day every muscle in Jack's body ached as he limped onto the plantation. A few more days of this and he might be dead. Either that or he would start to get used to it—whichever one came first. All day long he cut stalks, bending and straightening, bending and straightening, until the muscles in his back screamed with pain. Toward noon he again met up with Diane. They talked furtively as they worked. "Did you know they worship these things?" Jack said. "Yes," she replied, "I found that very interesting. They are also not allowed to read."

"Sounds a lot like a cult, doesn't it?"

"Complete with an intense regimen of brainwashing," Diane noted. "From infancy, they are read stories about the nephilim. Told how great they are. Over and over and over again."

"Like you said, brainwashing."

"But it goes beyond even that. It's more like . . . a spell. If these creatures really have this much power, why the need to keep *convincing* these people that they have it? Why do they have to drill it into them from birth? And what about those stupid glasses. Why can't they show their eyes?"

"I thought that was strange, too."

"And another thing," Diane said. "They build this whole thing around one verse—Genesis 6:4. It says: "The Nephilim were on the earth in those days, and also afterward, when the sons of God came in to the daughters of men, and they bore children to them. Those were the mighty men who were of old, men of renown." It doesn't mean literal giants. It means men of great renown. There are no nephilim."

"Someone needs to tell these people that," Jack said.

"Yeah, you got that right. But when? How?"

"How about Sunday, in the temple?"

"They wouldn't let us speak," Diane said.

"They would if it was to praise them. They allow slaves to offer testimony in the temple. Testimony to their greatness, of course. Maybe you could go up there and give these people a little history lesson instead."

Jack noticed a guard watching them from the sides. "We better disperse," he said, "We'll talk again tomorrow."

And so the days went by, each one like the last, like re-occurring images in a bad dream, filled with back breaking toil in the scorching sun, under the grim glare of the nephilim, until Sunday finally rolled around. Their day off. Jack and Sawyer were dressed in their Sunday best. The slaves were allowed to wear suits to the temple instead of their slave uniforms. "How do I look?" Sawyer asked, adjusting his tie. "Just great," Jack said. Moments later they filed out of the barracks, along with some of the other slaves, and into the bus, which took them to the midtown temple—the largest temple in town. Two other buses were already there, in the parking lot.

As they filed in, Jack looked around for Diane, and spotted her up front. He went and sat down next to her. The temple was huge, with four rows of pews; two large ones in the middle, and two smaller ones on the ends. An aisle ran up the center, leading up to the pulpit, which featured two lecterns, one to the right and one to he left, and in the center an altar. The nephilim, it seemed, had adopted most of the trappings of Catholicism, and their temple and service were patterned on that model. The service began with songs of praise, continued with some announcements, and concluded with a sermon by the priest. The sermon, though, was not a sermon at all; rather it was a fabricated tale revolving around the nephilim, designed to emphasize their greatness and heroism. After that, the priest—Father Daley—asked if anyone would like to come forth and present their personal testimonies. Several slaves, including Diane, raised their hand. One by one the priest called them forward, where they stood behind the lectern and proceeded to heap praise upon the nephilim.

Then the priest called on Diane. She squeezed Jack's hand and headed up to the lectern. "Thank you, Father Daley," she said, "And thank you to all of you." She spread her hands out toward the congregation. "I'm new here, but I want to say that being here, and having the chance to serve the nephilim has truly been an extraordinary experience. I wasn't familiar with the story of the nephilim, as you all are. But I grew up in a religious family, and I do remember the verse my mother read to me about the great nephilim: "There were giants in the earth in those days; and also after that, when the sons of God came in unto the daughters of men, and they bare children to them, the same became mighty men which were of old, men of renown."

"Wow, what a verse," Diane said. "In the Hebrew it goes . . ." She proceeded to recite the verse in Hebrew, pronouncing each word flawlessly. The congregation gasped. Very few slaves could even *read* the scripture, much less translate it perfectly into Hebrew. She had gotten their attention, and, more than that, their respect. They were hanging on her words now. They were *open* to what she had to say. Jack remembered what she said the other day, about the people being under a spell, and about how she had to break it, how she had to find a way to *convince* them. Well, now she had set the stage to do exactly that.

"The great thing about scripture," she continued, "is that there are so many ways to interpret it. Most people look at the words *When the sons of God came into the daughters of men, and bare children to them*, and they think this is talking about Gods having sex with humans and having children—called nephilim." She paused and smiled. "But we know this is impossible, for Genesis 1:24 says *everything* reproduces *after its own kind!*" Gasps went up from the congregation.

"So, what is the verse really saying?" Diane continued. "The phrase *the sons of God* simply means *people who had become saved*, not Gods; that's what it means *every other time it's used in the bible*, and that's what it means here."

She began to hurry her words as a church official began to approach her, apparently with the intent of dragging her off the stage. "And when we read it that way, it makes more sense. The men in view were not Gods, not

God-human hybrids; just men of great renown. That's the *truth,* people; you have been told a lie, and the lie doesn't like the *light,* because the light *exposes* it."

More gasps went up from the crowd as the official put a hand on Diane's shoulder, about to grab her away. As she did, she shouted, "A lie cannot bear the light," and tore the nephilims glasses off, revealing two bulbous, red orbs, filled with veins, that began to writhe around wildly in their sockets, the capillaries straining, as if they might burst at any moment. The nephilm shrieked in pain, covering his eyes with his hands as he slumped to the canvas. "You see," Diane shouted into the microphone, "They are not Gods at all; they are just men!" As she spoke those words she pointed to the slumping figure, and all eyes fixed on him. And it was not the figure of a God, or a nephilim. It was the figure of an ordinary man, of ordinary size, slumped on the floor, rubbing his eyes furiously. The people gasped in disbelief, turning their gaze to the priest, who also turned into an ordinary man right before their eyes.

Jack walked up to Diane and gave her a hug. "I guess the spell is broken," he said. "I guess so," Diane replied, as the people flooded around them, thanking them, hugging them, bombarding them with a mixture of approbation and questions.

The questions were all answered in due time. Jack and Diane stood in San Milo for another two days. During that time a lot of things changed. At first, the former slaves were furious. They wanted blood. Fortunately, cooler heads prevailed and there was no bloodshed. Instead an agreement was reached: a housing project would commence immediately, with the goal of building homes for all the former slaves. In the meantime, some of them would share the homes of their former slave masters, while some would continue to live in the barracks. They would continue to do their jobs, but with three stipulations: eight-hour work days, fair compensation, and access to education. Moreover, they would marry and raise their own children, and each slave would receive ten thousand dollars in reparations.

In the meantime, a great feast was held at the San Milo stadium in honor of the town liberators, Jack and Diane. Eternally grateful, the citizens of San Milo offered them anything they wanted. They settled for ten thousand dollars in cash and a new car. As the celebration wound to a close, Sawyer escorted them out of the stadium, where their new car, a 2017 Mercedes, awaited them in the parking lot. By this time, they had figured out that he had been there guide for this last journey—the land of the nephilim.

As they prepared to leave San Milo behind them, Jack asked Sawyer, "So, what's next? Can you tell us?"

"I can, but you ain't gonna like it."

"Come on, what is it? What's the next city?"

"Not a city so much as a . . . place."

"What place?"

As Sawyer walked away he just sort of mumbled the answer in a barely audible tone. But as they looked at each other's face, each reading the horror in the other's eyes, Jack and Diane both knew they had heard him correctly when he had muttered the solitary four letter word *hell*.

20

"California, here we come," Jack shouted as they got onto 99. "Won't be long now," Diane said, "'bout another hundred miles."

"So, what are you going to do first when we get there?" Jack asked.

"I don't know, I've never been there," Diane replied.

"That makes the two of us."

"I know what I want to do now," Diane said, "I want to stop at a motel and take a nap."

"Me too," Jack agreed. His tone was light, but there was a heaviness in his chest. Sawyer's words were still with him, like the after taste of a bad meal. *Hell*. According to him, that's where they were headed, and Jack didn't like the sound of that one bit. A part of him wished they had left well enough alone and just stayed forever in the land of the snake people, in their own private palace, with no cares and no worries. Maybe it was just a dream world, but what was better—a wonderful dream or a nightmarish reality?

Diane turned off an exit for a rest stop that advertised a Motel 6. Moments later she pulled into the lot. It was a small motel, one level, with about a dozen rooms and an office off to the left. They grabbed their backpacks and went into the office. "Good evening, folks," the man behind the counter said, "What can I do for you today?" He was a small fellow, bent over, with a slight hump in his back, and he walked with a bit of a shuffle. He had thinning black hair, combed over his forehead in bangs, a large nose, and dim looking blue eyes. On his shirt was a tag with the name CARSON on it.

"We'd like a room," Jack said, leaning up against the counter. "Sure thing," the man said. "How long will you be staying?"

"Overnight," Jack said.

"Sign here," Carson said, pointing to the registry. "That'll be ninety bucks." Jack paid the man. "Thank you, sir," Carson said, then grabbed a key off of a hook on the wall, and handed it to Jack. "There you are, enjoy your stay."

"Thank you," Jack said, taking the key. He and Diane left the office, turned left, and made their way down the row of rooms to the one that matched the number on the key—7. Then he opened the door. The room was nicer than he expected. It was large and clean, with a fresh smell that was kind of a mixture of pine and Lysol. It was laid out like most motel rooms: bed on one wall, with night stands on either side, and lamps on the night stands; a TV opposite the bed on a dresser; an arm chair on the far wall, near the window; a closet and bathroom to the left of the entrance, and a desk in the corner.

They tossed their back packs on the bed and unpacked the few items they had, placing some cloths in dressers, and some toiletries in the bathroom. When they were finished, they showered, Diane first, then Jack. When Jack came out of the shower Diane was still in her bathrobe, lying on the bed, her head and neck propped up against the head board. One of her legs was folded up at the knee, the other stretched out on the bed. She had a coy grin on her face, and when she caught his eye, she loosened the belt on her bathrobe, and let it open up a little.

Jack felt himself growing hard beneath his towel. He took it off and slid into bed with her. Her fresh-from-the-shower scent filled his nostrils. She cupped his chin in her hand and brought her face slowly toward his, puckering her lips as she approached. She stopped an inch before their lips met, letting the anticipation build, until he could stand it no longer, and then touched his lips softly with her own. But she did not kiss him deeply, not yet. Instead she pecked around the edges of his lips, tickling him, her breath warm on his skin, as the anticipation continued to build. Then, when he could stand it no longer, she placed her lips squarely on his, without moving them, and pressed. Then, and only then, did she enter his mouth with her tongue, moving it around in a slow, circular pattern. Then she slid her arms around his back and drew him down on top of her and inside of her. She wrapped her legs around him, feet pressing his buttocks, as he began to thrust, first slowly, then faster. Jack could literally feel himself throbbing inside of her, like he was going to explode. A wave of pleasure was rising in him of an intensity literally a hundred times greater than anything he had ever experienced before—even in his *dreams*. He felt like a man about to be swallowed by a thousand-foot high tidal wave and he began to whimper with a mixture of anticipation, ecstasy, and even fright.

He looked into Diane's eyes and saw that she could see what he was feeling. She just smiled warmly and whispered, "It's okay; just let it go." Her voice was quivering; she was feeling it too, as the wave, the likes of which was beyond imagining, was about to sweep them both away.

And then she did something which, if possible, made it even more intense: she shoved her tongue deep in his mouth and began rolling it around. As the wave hit, racking their entwined bodies with spasms of tortured ecstasy, Jack had that feeling again—like they were melting into each other. Only this time, Diane did not stop it. Jack almost wished that she would, so intense was the sensation. As it continued, he felt himself losing all sense of time and space. No longer were they making loving to each other merely with two hands and two feet and two sets of lips, but rather with their entire beings, devoid of any limitations of any kind, as they entered a different kind of world—one of spirit. Jack could feel a thousand hands on him all at once, exploring every corner of his body, suffusing his entire being, his every molecule, with unthinkable pleasure. And yet every hand was Diane. And not just hands, but her feet, her scent, her breath; all of her was everywhere all at once, filling him, tickling him, caressing him, until he literally screamed with pleasure.

When it was over, Jack was limp, his body, mind, and soul spent, as if someone had opened him up, turned him upside down, and poured out every ounce of energy in his being. He fell into sleep like someone falling into a chair.

～

When Jack woke up the next morning the place on the bed next to him was empty. *She must be in the bathroom*, he thought, tossing the sheets off. He sat on the edge of the bed, yawned, and stretched himself out. Last night was exhilarating, exhausting, and even, in some ways, terrifying. He was surprised that he did not feel more tired, more drained. But he didn't. He felt fine.

He went over to the dresser and took out his cloths. *Might as well get dressed while she's in bathroom*, he thought. He finished dressing and sat on the edge of the bed, waiting for Diane to finish up. Peering at the bathroom, he noticed there was no light coming out from the slit under the door. "Diane?" he called out. No answer. He approached the door and knocked lightly. "Diane, are you in there?" Again, no answer. He felt a slight chill go down his spine. Where was she? *Calm down*, he told himself. She can't be far. Probably just needed something for the room and went to the office.

So that's where he headed, walking quickly, tossing the door to the office open and rushing toward the counter. Carson was behind it, seated at a desk, watching a morning show. He swiveled around in his chair when he saw Jack come in. "Good morning, sir," he said, "Are you checking out?"

"No," Jack said, "I was hoping you could help me with something. Have you seen the woman I came in with?"

"Diane? No, I haven't."

Jack could literally feel something sink in his stomach upon hearing those words. He had pinned his hopes on the possibility that she was here; where else could she be? She would not have left the premises without telling him.

"Jesus," Jack said, running a hand through his head and looking around nervously, as if she might pop out of a corner. "She's not in our room," he said, looking helplessly at the manager.

"Well, maybe she stepped out," he offered.

"She wouldn't do that without telling me," Jack replied.

"Is it possible she told you and you forgot?" Jack thought about that for a moment. Maybe she mentioned something, whispered it in his ear, and he forgot it. Or maybe she thought he heard him, but he didn't. Maybe, but it wasn't likely. And where would she go? There was nowhere here within walking distance, and the car was still there. No, that couldn't be it.

"That's not it," Jack said. "She must . . ." He stopped in mid-sentence and glared at Carson intently. "You called her Diane," he said. "I didn't tell you her name." Carson shrugged and threw his hands up. "You got me," he said. "I lied." Jack grabbed him by the shirt, pulled him forward, and shouted "Where is she? Tell me right now!"

"Hold on, hold on," he said, "Diane is just fine. Let go of me and I will tell you exactly where she is." Jack let go, but he was ready to spring again if he didn't like the answer. "First, allow me to introduce myself," the man said, extending a hand. "I am Carson, your guide for the sixth city—Hell."

Jack stared at him in disbelief, although at this point perhaps nothing should have surprised him. "Okay," Jack said, feeling a slight twinge of relief that at least now he had *some* kind of an answer. "But you didn't answer the question; where is Diane?"

"I'm surprised you didn't figure it out for yourself," Carson said, sounding disappointed.

"Figure what out?" Jack demanded.

"Where she is?" Carson continued. "You did join with her last night, didn't you?" Jack was too upset to be embarrassed that this man, or whatever he was, apparently knew the intimate details of his encounter with Diane last night. Setting aside his pride, he said simply "Yes."

"Well, there's your answer," Carson said. "The two of you are now one."

"What?" Jack barked. "That's insane! I made love to her; I didn't *consume* her." But even as he spoke he remembered how Diane had always stopped him before they reached that point during previous encounters, as if it would cause something terrible to happen, and instantly he knew that Carson had told him the truth. "My God!" he said, leaning up against the counter for support, placing his head in his hand. "How could this be?" he asked, looking at Carson helplessly.

"How can I explain this?" Carson sighed. "You never really were interested in this mission. But you were interested in her. You wanted *her*. Her job was to get you going. And she did. And in the process, she made you better. Think about it. You're selfish, she's selfless; you're lazy, she's diligent; you're sloppy, she's meticulous; you're closed minded, she's open-minded. But now, you are better than when you started. More like her. And she's the reason. She is your other half. Remember, in the garden Adam and Eve started out as *one*. Then God took a rib out of Adam, and made Eve, because *it was not good for him to be alone*. And that's how it was with you. It was not good for you to be alone on this mission. You needed help. So, God gave you Diane. But she was never meant to exist independently of you. She was meant to exist in relation to you, until you were ready to finish the mission on your own. And now you are."

"But I'm not!" Jack cried. "I can't finish it without Diane. I can't even *live* without Diane!"

"I'm sorry," Carson shrugged, "But I don't make the rules."

"Well . . . can't you help me? Talk to someone! I need her back!" Jack was almost in tears now. But Carson just shrugged. "I'm sorry, chief. There's nothing I can do."

A thousand objections flooded Jack's mind, and he was tempted to let them all pour forth like water at Carson until he relented and reversed his stand. But he knew it would not do any good. Whoever and whatever these guides were, one thing had become abundantly clear: they could do only as they were told, no more no less. Their boundaries were as marked out for them as those of man, or any other creature, and there was no changing them. So, Jack did not try. He just sighed and said "So, now what? What am I supposed to do?"

Carson's face flushed; he looked embarrassed by how little help he was permitted to give. "I am sorry," he said, "But I cannot tell you that. I don't even know it myself."

Jack just stood there, staring at him, hoping against hope there was something, *anything* he could say to ease the absolute nightmare that had consumed him at this moment. But he knew there was nothing he could do, and after a few more moments, he simply left the office and headed back for his motel room.

For a few moments Jack just paced the room, still not quite comprehending what had happened, still half expecting Diane to come out of the bathroom or walk through the front door. But as the minutes passed, and it didn't happen, the reality of it all became clear. She was gone. Once and for all. And she was never coming back. Jack slumped to his knees, his head resting on the edge of the bed, and began to sob. He sobbed uncontrollably. For a while, he thought he might never stop. He just thought he might sob until all of the moisture just passed out of his body, leaving him lying there on the floor like a desiccated roach. And that would have been fine with him, because he didn't have the slightest desire to go on alone. But eventually the tears did stop, although he knew they would return soon, and he dragged himself off the floor and began packing his things.

⌒

The hours went by. They turned into days. The days turned into weeks. And the weeks into months. Jack went back to his old life, drifting from town to town, taking menial jobs, sleeping in flophouses, on park benches, and in cheap motels. The searing pain of the loss of Diane slowly transformed into a constant, dull throbbing, which he medicated continuously with a steady flow of drugs and alcohol. The mission became a memory. Eventually, he became convinced that he had imagined the whole thing.

After a few months had passed he found himself working as a waiter at a strip club outside Sacramento. The place was called The Jiggle Room, and the people there were like him—lost souls just trying to survive. It was during an encounter with one such soul, a stripper, that he reached a turning point. They were in the alley beside the club, sitting up against the wall, doing lines of cocaine. "Come on, hold it still Joyce," Jack said. "I'm trying," Joyce laughed, "your hands are too shaky." Joyce had the coke lines laid out on the surface of her opened lipstick mirror. "*My* hands," Jack said, "You're the one holding the mirror."

She laughed and nudged him with her shoulder. "Come on, be serious," Jack said, putting the straw to the coke, holding one nostril, and sniffing it up. "Oh, yeah," he sighed, leaning his head up against the wall, as the feeling washed through him. When he went in for another sniff, he saw that it was all gone and said, "Oh, shit, we used it all up!"

"Don't worry, hon," she said, reaching into the cleavage of her blouse and pulling out another vial, "We got more." She opened the vial and started pouring it onto the mirror. "Oh, I could kiss you," Jack said, and then did just that, giving her a quick peck on the cheek. He started to feel aroused, the way he often did when he snorted coke. He stared leeringly at Joyce. She was old for a stripper—almost forty—and too thin, but she had nice tits and a pretty face, long and angular, with thin, delicate features, and big, blue eyes. She was wearing a short black skirt, black stockings and matching pumps, with a tight, low cut blouse that showed off her ample bosom quite nicely.

She started cutting up the coke with a credit card, arranging it into lines. As she did Jack was sliding a hand down her leg. "Hey, did you want to get high or make out?" she asked, not looking up from her work. "I was hoping we could do both," Jack said.

As he spoke he realized they were not alone. Two more people, a man and a woman, had occupied spots on the other end of the alley, one on each side. They were leaning against the wall, legs spread out in front of them. The alley was accessible at both ends, so they must have come in from the other side, as Jack had not noticed them walk by. The man was drinking from a flask; the women was just sitting there, rubbing her hands together. Their presence made Jack uneasy, but he tried to ignore it.

He turned his attention back to Joyce and started nibbling on her ear as she took a snort. Then she turned to him, smiled wickedly, and slowly licked her lips with her tongue. He leaned in and kissed her on the mouth. "Mmmm," she said, then blew the rest of the coke off the mirror, snapped it shut, and put it back in her bag. Then she turned herself sideways a bit, facing Jack, and put a hand on his chest. She started moving it around, slowly, in circles, as she moved her face closer to his, her lips pursed. As she did Jack could hear more noise in the alley; apparently the place was popular tonight. He tried to ignore it, concentrating on Joyce, as he moved in to kiss her. Their lips touched. But as their tongues probed Jack felt a sudden pinching on his, as if he had been stabbed, and when he withdrew, suddenly Joyce's tongue was forked and quivering, like that of a snake's. Jack leapt back with a start. *What the fuck?* For a few seconds everything went blank, then Joyce was saying, "Are you okay?"

"What?" he asked.

She looked at him askance. "I said, are you okay? You sort of freaked out on me for a second."

Jack realized that he had imagined it. Joyce was fine. It was just a fleeting, drug-induced brain fart that altered his perception of reality for one second. Nothing to get upset about.

But he was upset.

"You all right, hon?" the woman leaning against the wall asked. She was middle aged, with a large gap in her mouth where her front teeth used to be. She was wearing a skirt, with leggings underneath, and two sweaters; on her head was a kerchief, and on her hands a pair of gloves with the fingers cut out. She was rubbing them together and smiling her semi toothless smile. "Um . . . Yeah, I'm fine," Jack said. "He's fine!" the man with the flask snarled, then looked at Jack and laughed.

"Come on, don't worry about *them*," Joyce said, turning his head back to face her. "Just concentrate all your attention on me."

But Jack's attention was waning fast. And as Joyce spoke those words two more people passed them by and found spots for themselves along the alley walls. This place was getting too close for comfort. Jack's heart was starting to race, and it wasn't from the coke. At least that wasn't the *only* reason. "Come on," Joyce said, pulling him to her, "Kiss me again." Again, he was in her mouth and again he felt the pinch. He withdrew, and just like the last time, her tongue was that of a snake, forked and quivering. But this time she didn't change back, at least not right away. She just stood there, wagging her snake tongue for him, as if it would be a turn on. "Don't you like it?" she asked.

"*I* like it," one of the newcomers to the alley shouted—a young woman with a bottle of beer in her hand, leaning up against the opposite wall. She wore a light leather jacket, jeans, and a pair of brown, knee high boots, one of which rested against the wall. She looked at Jack and winked. She looked strangely familiar. All of them did.

"That's okay," Joyce said, putting her finger under Jack's chin. "I don't have to do the tongue thing." Then she tilted her head and smiled a charming, innocent smile, and said, "Okay? No more games." Jack suspected it was too late for that, but again he found himself being drawn in by her charms. She grabbed a handful of his jacket and pulled him on top of her, straddling him with her legs. Then she put a hand around his head and brought his face slowly down to her own. But with each inch that she drew him closer, she began to change. Her skin, young and smooth, started to crease and crack; her lips, soft and supple, started to dry out like prunes; her eyes, bright and clear, became two bulbous red orbs; her teeth, straight and white, became black and covered with film. By the time his lips touched hers, she was a moldy, stench-ridden, old hag. "No!" he shouted, drawing back and trying to escape her grip. But she latched on hard, tightening her grip and pulling him in. Their lips met, and he gagged on her putrid breath. Finally, he managed to pry her arms off his head and break free. He scrambled to his feet. When he looked down at her, she was just Joyce again, looking up at him curiously.

"What's wrong?" the young woman with beer bottle asked. "You don't like girls?"

And then he recognized her. It was Sally Sanders. In fact, he recognized the others, too. The woman by the garbage can was his mother; the man opposite was his father. And as he looked around the alley was filling up with more people that he recognized: a woman came hobbling by on crutches—the woman from the land of the nephilim; a man came by pointing at him and laughing—it was Carson; a huge man with iron teeth—the Slave Master; one by one people from his past filled the alley, crowding in on him, laughing, hurling insults, pelting him with objects, until he was forced into the corner, hands raised over his head, trying to defend himself against the onslaught. But it was no use; there were too many; he began to slump, in sections, down to the ground, like a boxer falling under the weight of a furious barrage.

And then, suddenly, they were gone, all except one—Carson—who stood at the foot of the alley and said, "I told you this was hell" then raised a hand, sending flames shooting up from all of the garbage cans in the alley. Jack watched helplessly as the flames crawled up onto the walls and made a circle around Jack, crackling all around him. It was like the blast from a furnace, and he cried out with pain. Slowly the circle of flames tightened, closing in on him. He stood there in the middle of the alley, preparing to be devoured alive, and he screamed.

He was still screaming as he saw Joyce's face, staring down at him, as she knelt over him and slapped him, softly and repeatedly. "Snap out of it," she said, "You're tripping."

Jack looked around. The woman and the man were still in the alley, but no-one else. He rose to his feet, his legs shaky. "Are you okay?" Joyce asked, placing an arm on his shoulder. Jack wasn't okay, but he lied and said, "Yeah, I'm fine."

"Are you sure?"

"I'm fine," Jack said. Without saying another word, he left the alley, got into his car, and drove across town, to the room he rented for two hundred dollars a month from a couple that made their money from a combination of welfare and dealing drugs. He went in through the back door, as he always did, and immediately flopped down on the sofa. The place wasn't much, but for a go nowhere drifter looking for a place to flop, it was a great set up. He had all he needed there; a sofa that pulled out into a bed, a TV, an entertainment center, a dresser and a snack tray. That was his life. At least it had been. It was not going to be his life anymore. He had made up his mind.

He got up from the sofa and went over to the dresser. He opened the bottom draw, pushed away some cloths, and took out his glock. Then he went back to the sofa and sat down, his knuckles white on the glock, and his hand trembling. He did not intend to draw this out. No suicide note. No last will and testament. No good byes. No last-minute trips down memory lane. He didn't even need to check the chamber; he knew it was fully loaded. So, he closed his eyes, shoved the gun in his mouth, and started to squeeze the trigger. Just as the gun was about to fire, he felt a tug on his arm, and suddenly the barrel of the glock was not in his mouth anymore. He turned to his right and there, seated beside him on the sofa, was Diane, her hand around the wrist that held the glock. She just stared at him, her brown eyes bigger than ever, and welled up with tears. She just whispered in a soft, quivering voice "Oh, Jack." A single, pear shaped tear slid slowly down her cheek. She was wearing a white dress, and her hair spilled down around her shoulders. Her legs were positioned closely together, knees touching, and one of her hands was resting on her thigh. On her feet were a pair of blue low-heeled shoes with the toes open. Jack just stared at her, breathless. "This is a trip," he said in a weak, quivering voice. Then, a little louder "That's all this is. I'm just tripping."

Diane gently took the gun out of his hand and placed it on the bed. Then she traced his face with her hand, ending at his chin, with she cupped in her palm, and said, "No, Jack. I'm here to take you out of hell."

And then she looked at the door, which was bathed in a shaft of gold light, and said, "I'm here to take you out of hell and into the land of the Cherubim." She took his hand and stood up. He stood up, too. Then she led him to the door, her eyes locked on his, and opened it. They were bathed in golden light as they walked through to the other side.

21

As Jack looked around, he had the distinct feeling of weightlessness, as if he were floating. He also had a sense of great peace, like nothing there could hurt him. He just wasn't too sure where *there* was. The place, whatever it was, consisted entirely of empty space. It was as if he had entered an immense, but completely empty, room—one without any walls, floors, or ceilings. "Where are we?" he asked Diane. "I told you," she answered, "The land of the Cherubim."

"But there's nothing here," Jack said.

"What do you want to be here?" Diane asked.

"I don't know," Jack said. "Anything. How about a floor for us to stand on?" No sooner had Jack spoken the words than a floor appeared beneath their feet. It was nothing fancy—just a plain, yellow linoleum floor. Jack looked at it, then looked back at Diane. "How did that happen?" he asked, glad to be back on the ground, but more than a bit puzzled at the attendant circumstances. "You thought it," Diane said. Jack took a moment to let the import of that statement sink in, then said, "You mean I can think things into existence in this place?"

"Absolutely," she said.

"Holy shit!" Jack said, looking around at the empty space all around him, and awed by the thought that he could fill it up with anything he wanted. He felt like a kid in a candy store, waiting to decide what to get first. "So," he said, "I guess the question is: What do I want?"

"Yep," Diane smiled.

"Well, first off," Jack said, "I want a nicer floor than this one." No sooner had he spoken than the plain yellowish floor turned into one of dazzling colors and texture. "That's more like it," Jack said. "Great job," Diane said, "Now what about all this empty space?"

"Well, let's see," Jack said, staring about. "How about a nature scene?" he said. An instant later, the empty space was filled with a lush garden, teeming with vegetation, trees, and flowers, that stretched as far as the eye could see. The beauty of the scene was beyond anything Jack had ever conceived. It was as if something had leaped off the pages of a painting. The colors, the symmetry, the shapes, the shadows, the interplay of light and dark: everything was bright and sparkling and vivid and just plain perfect. "Incredible!" Jack said, gazing around in wonder at the magnificent landscape that had just popped out of his imagination.

"Hey, you're getting good at this," Diane said. "But where are we supposed to live? How about a house for us?" No sooner did she say it than Jack thought them a house. "I didn't know you liked log cabins," Diane said. "There's probably a lot you don't know about me," Jack replied, as they strolled together toward their new home, which was nestled in a woodsy area, surrounded by trees and shrubbery.

"I love it," Diane said, as they walked up the narrow cobblestone path that led to their front door. Jack held the door for her as they went inside. "Not bad," Diane observed, looking around. In the middle of the room, laid out in a square pattern, were a series of sofas and accent chairs, with a space rug in the middle. On one wall was a bear head over an antique, wood burning fireplace. On another was a rowboat. The walls were adorned with paintings of nature scenes that complimented the log cabin theme. "Not bad at all," Diane said. "Thanks," Jack said, "But I think it could use a woman's touch."

"Yes, I can see that," Diane said. She cut her eyes to the mostly empty kitchen. Seconds later it was filled with a large oak table and matching cabinets, along with wood colored counters and floor. "Nice," Jack said. "Now, let's work on the bedroom," Diane said, leading Jack down a hall off the living area, to the bedroom. As they entered the room Diane's eyes opened wide in astonishment. "Wow!" she gasped, then gave Jack a wry look. "I guess you don't need any help with this room, huh?"

"Well," Jack said shyly, "It is an important room." On one end of the room was a huge, slowly spinning waterbed, with a canopy over it. In the center of the room were several sofas and chairs. On one wall was an armoire; on another a dresser, and in the corner a vanity table with a mirror. The rug was an extra plush brown. Paintings adorned the walls.

"Very nicely done," Diane said, climbing, catlike, onto the bed, and sitting there, one leg folded beneath her. She looked coyly at Jack and patted the bed. Not needing to be asked twice, Jack joined her. By the time he did, she had already slipped out of her dress. "Come 'ere, you," she said, pulling him toward her, and taking off his shirt. Jack remembered the last time they made love, how it felt, and a nervous anticipation welled up inside of him. Sensing his concern, Diane said, "You don't have to worry about that here. Here we can do anything we want." Then she put her mouth to his ear and whispered, "Anything at all."

"That sounds good to me," Jack said, sliding his pants off.

"Good," Diane said, slipping out of her underwear. Then, getting on all fours, she whispered in his hear "So tell me, what do you want?"

"I want you," Jack said.

"I know *that*," she whispered, her breath tickling him, "But what else. *Who* else?"

"What do you mean?" Jack asked.

"I mean . . ." she said, cupping his chin with her hand and locking onto his eyes with her own "you can have *anything* here. No guilt."

"Well, I . . ." Jack stammered, but Diane silenced him quickly, putting a finger to his mouth. "Shhh!" she said, "I told you, no guilt. Here, I'll help you." She spread her arm out and suddenly they were not alone anymore. There with them, spread out on the bed in a variety of positions, was an assortment of no less than six other women, all scantily clothed, all young, all beautiful. Jack looked at them with disbelief, as they eyed him coyly. He looked at Diane, as if for help. She just smiled and slid behind him, wrapping her arms around his neck and her legs around his waist. Then she said, "Come on ladies. Let's share." As Diane breathed in his ear from behind, the bevy of beauties slowly converged upon him from the front. And for the next hour they took him new and unimagined heights of ecstasy. When it was over, Diane snapped her fingers and they were gone. "Don't worry," Diane teased, "you can have them back any time you want. But for now, I want you all to myself." Then she wrapped herself around him and the two of them drifted off to sleep.

The days went by and they filled the land with more things every day, building their own wonderland, complete with everything they had ever wanted or even *could* want. Jack was having so much fun that he had not bothered to ascertain the precise details about this place—what it was, or how it related to their mission, or even if they still had a mission. And part of him, in truth, did not want to know, for he remembered well that the last time he had discovered paradise and asked questions, the answers led him to leave it behind—and wind up in hell. And so, for a long while he was content to enjoy his new surroundings, in the company of the woman he loved, without asking questions, the answers to which he might not like. But as it usually does, curiosity began to get the better of him, and one day, while Diane was otherwise occupied, he took a stroll to the library and did some research. He walked straight to the card catalog and pulled out the drawer marked C through D. He noted the location of books on Cherubim and made his way to that aisle. He quickly found a number of books on the subject. He grabbed a handful and brought them over to a table, where he sat down and did some research. Of particular interest was the definition of the word Cherubim: an imaginary creature. At about the same time, something jogged in his memory—a verse from the bible which, for some reason or another, he had not remembered until that moment. He could not remember it exactly, but it pertained to Cherubim. So, he went back to the shelves, found a bible, and returned to the table. He searched the bible for the verse. It was, "So he drove out the man, and he placed at the east of the garden of Eden Cherubims, and a flaming sword which turned every way, to keep the way of the tee of life."

He thought the findings were interesting, if not disturbing. He closed the books and returned them to their proper place on the shelves. Then he went home, where he found Diane waiting for him, sitting by the fire in their living room.

"Hi, hon," she said. "Where have you been?"

"At the library," he replied, sitting down next to her. "Doing some research." She sidled up to him, resting her chin on his shoulder, and folding her legs beneath her buttocks. "About what?" she asked.

"About this place we live in."

"What about it?" she asked, nibbling his ear.

"It's not real, is it?" he asked. Diane sighed and said, "Define reality."

"And you are not real either," he said. "This is all a glorious fantasy designed to keep me from leaving and going back to Eden."

"And what do you think is waiting for you there?" Diane asked. "Do you think Eden is a garden, filled with lush flowers and animals and beauty? Well, it's not. That's what *this* is. Eden is nothing but pain."

"Yes, but it is also the real world. It is truth. And I was meant to lead the world to truth, and out of error. And I can't do that if I stay here, suspended in a fantasy."

"You know, Jack," she whispered, her breath tickling his ear, "Some philosophers don't even believe there's a difference between reality and fantasy. There's only mind and what we fill it with."

"Do you believe that, Diane?" he asked, somehow knowing that she would not lie to him, maybe because in his mind she *couldn't* lie to him.

"Let me ask you something," she said, "Would you rather live in a glorious fantasy or a hellish reality?" He did not answer her. The two said nothing for several moments. Then Diane took Jack by the hand and led him over to the door. She opened it and pointed out into the distance. Jack followed the trajectory of her finger. Out in the distance, beyond the wonderful world in which they lived, was another world. Buildings rose in the distance, drab and colorless. It was the real world. "That's Eden," Diane said. "You can go back any time you want. But you will have to leave everything else behind. Including me."

They went back inside. They spent the rest of the day together, sampling all of the pleasures that surrounded them, and creating new ones as they desired, like magicians in the world's greatest sci-fi fantasy. When it was over, they retired to their room, where they fell asleep quickly.

The next morning Jack woke up at dawn. He walked over to their bedroom window and opened the blinds, letting the morning sunshine wash over him. Then he got dressed and walked over to the bed, where Diane lie on her side, sleeping peacefully. He stared at her for several moments, then bent down, brushed the long blonde hair away from her face, and kissed her on the cheek. Then he left the bedroom and walked down the stairs, making as little noise as possible, so as not to wake her.

The morning light stung his eyes as he stepped out onto the front porch and shut the door behind him. Then he began walking. He walked past the green meadows, the lush rose beds, the sparkling streams, the sprawling fields, until he reached the place where the colors faded, and the light dimmed, and the air grew thicker. He stood there for a moment, as if suspended by an invisible tether, and then, without looking back, he entered. And instantly he was back in his apartment, sitting on the bed, with his glock beside him on the mattress. He had made it. He had gotten through all seven cities. It occurred to him that Diane must have been his guide for the last one. And now, here he was, back in the real world, stripped of all illusions, lies, and selfish fantasies, with the task still before him: how to lead the world back to the garden of Eden.

PART 3

EDEN

.

22

HIS FIRST INSTINCT WAS to flop down on the sofa and take a nap. After all, he had just made it through the last of the seven cities; didn't he deserve a break? Maybe he did, but he wasn't going to take one. Not now. He had already wasted too much time; he wasn't going to waste one more second. So, he sat down at his desk, opened a draw, and pulled out a spiral notebook. In it were the notes he been keeping since the mission started three months ago. He turned on his laptop and clicked on the Microsoft Word application, opening up a new document. At the top of the page, in bold letters, he typed the title: *The Tree Within*. And then he started writing the story of he and Diane's journey from Silverton, Illinois to Sacramento, California, and everywhere and everything in between.

He was not the world's best writer, but somehow the words just came to him, and when they did he captured them on the screen, one by one, until he had completed the entire book. It took him one month. He would go to work each day, then come home and write. No more drugs, no more alcohol, no more whoring around. All he did was work, sleep, eat, and write. Five hours a day after work and all day on his days off. He wrote and wrote and wrote until the story was finished.

But writing the book was only half the battle. Getting it published was the other half—and it was just as difficult and time consuming as the first. Each publisher wanted a different type of proposal, and he wound up spending as much time preparing proposals as he had on the book itself. But eventually, he hammered out some decent proposals and fired them off to publishers, at a rate of about two or three a day. Some of the responses came quickly; others took some time. But they were all the same: brief, but polite letters informing him that his book, while interesting, did not suit their particular tastes, but he should keep on trying, maybe someone else would like it. He began to think that maybe he had wasted his time writing a book. Indeed, he started to think that maybe he had wasted his time accepting the mission in the first place. He started to wish he had just stayed in the land of the Cherubim, lost in his blissful reverie with the woman he loved—real or not—forever.

But that all changed on day in mid-December. Jack came home from his shift, tired and sore, and sat down at his desk. He tuned his lap top on and checked his email. In the *From* line was the name of a man—Stanton Dozier—and in the *Subject* line were the words *Offer Of Publication*.

"Holy shit!" Jack whispered, his eyes wide and his heart fluttering. He clicked on the line and opened the email. As it happened, Mr. Dozier was an editor at Putnam Books. He read Jack's book and he loved it. Not only did he want to publish it, but he offered Jack an advance of a hundred thousand dollars!

Jack quickly accepted the offer, and, almost as quickly, he had his hundred thousand dollars. He used the money to move from his little one room hovel to a nice apartment in Sacramento.

A few months after that the book was published to rave reviews. Sales were brisk, and before long the pithy little tome that this first-time author had hammered out in his garage apartment had become a full-fledged, break out best seller. People were fascinated by this allegedly factual account of a young couple's mystical journey through seven cities on their way to finding the way back to the garden of Eden. Although not everyone accepted the incredible claims the book made—in fact some believed it was thinly veiled fiction—it had managed to ignite a theological firestorm. Religious liberals hailed it as a clarion call to a new understanding of God, while conservatives derided it as pure heresy. For the most part, Jack had not joined the debate, preferring instead to simply let the book speak for itself, and to talk about his own beliefs and experiences as he appeared on rounds and rounds of talk and radio shows.

But that was about to change. Kelly Carter, the host of a highly rated national talk show, which featured a highly confrontational format, with audience participation, was doing a show entitled *What Is God Like?* and she wanted Jack to be one of the guests. The other guest would be Calvin Connors, an old-fashioned fire and brimstone preacher with his own radio show and a pretty large following.

Jack jumped at the chance. Although he was no bible expert, he remembered a lot from his childhood, and had learned a lot more over the past few months, and he felt he could hold his own. More than that, he knew the exposure would be great for book sales. Before he knew it, the day of the taping had arrived, and he found himself sitting backstage in the greenroom, waiting to be introduced. Fidgeting, he watched on a screen backstage as the pretty blonde host introduced Calvin first, with the words: *My first guest is the host of the WKMP morning program* God Watch *and author of a new book called* God's Not Santa Claus: Reclaiming God. *He feels that too many people these days, including our next guest, are misrepresenting the character of God, presenting Him as a Santa Claus, rather than the holy and sovereign ruler of our universe. Ladies and gentlemen—Calvin Connors.*

The mostly liberal leaning crowd applauded politely as Calvin took the stage and shook hands with Kelly. He was an older man—mid-sixties—with white hair and a mustache; he wore a finely tailored grey suit, with a handkerchief poking out of the pocket. He looked relaxed and confident.

Next, she introduced Jack with the words: "*Our next guest is Jack Horn, the author of The Tree Within. I read this book and I love it. He makes a lot of points in his book, and we'll discuss some of them with him. Ladies and gentlemen—Jack Horn.*"

The stage was set—literally. Jack sat on one side; Calvin on the other. The host, wearing a knee length powder blue dress and matching pumps, sat, legs crossed, in between them. She started with Calvin. "Mr. Connor, your book is entitled *God's Not Santa Claus.* You think Mr. Horn is one of the people out there who portrays God as Santa Claus. How so?"

"Well, in a lot of ways," Calvin said, "But before I even talk about that I want to talk a little about his book first. It was very creative and he's obviously a very clever young man. But it's dangerous to disguise fiction as nonfiction; there's a lot of impressionable people out there. And many of them will really believe this stuff actually happened. And they will also believe everything he says about God—things that aren't true."

"You know, I'm glad you mentioned that," Kelly said, "because I did a little fact checking and we were actually able to verify one of the more incredible things in the book."

She turned to the audience, addressing them. "There's a chapter in there that revolves around a city called San Milo, in Utah. He says the people there were under a spell and being used as slaves. Well, we sent a team of investigators to San Milo to speak to the residents there, and they verified every word in his book."

The audience erupted with applause. "Yep," Kelly continued, "and a few of them are here today." She pointed to three people in the front row and said, "Stand up." Jack was astonished as he watched two people from the town stand up; he recognized both of them. The third did not stand up; she was in a wheelchair. It was the woman they had rescued, whose leg had been amputated. Jack gave them a big wave, and they waved back. Calvin shrank in his seat as Kelly introduced the three people, then asked the woman "Was he making any of this up?"

"Not a word," the woman proudly replied. "It all happened exactly the way he said it did." Again, the audience erupted.

From there it was all downhill for Calvin, who could only go through the motions for the rest of the show, making his points with all the conviction of someone trying to sell stag films at a convent. Toward the end Jack went in for the kill by saying: "Look, we can argue about scripture all day long. You could throw this verse at me and I could throw that verse at you; it's called bible boxing and it will get us nowhere. So, let me just close by giving you what I have come to call The Twelve Points: They are twelve points that comprise the narrative of the gospel as its presented by the Christian Religious System. If you can tell me how the last one, by any standard of logic, reason, or philosophy, can be reconciled to the first eleven, I will bow down before you here on this stage, and beg your forgiveness. Is that fair enough?"

His face drained of color, Calvin said simply "Fair enough." Then Jack gave his twelve points, citing chapter and verse for each one:

God is love

Out of love He created us

He created us in His image

He declared us very good

He is our Father

He created us for Himself

He declared jealous ownership of us

He died for our sins

He justified us

He wants us to be saved

He draws us

He will torture most of us in hell forever

And when he had finished, he leaned forward and asked Connor: "Well, can you do it? Can you reconcile the last point with the first eleven?"

Connor, desperately trying to salvage the last vestiges of his dignity, tried to mount a response, but Jack had a clear and decisive rebuttal for everything he had to say. In the end he looked like a fool and Jack like a hero. And the crowd actually gave Jack a standing ovation.

After that appearance the sales of The Tree Within skyrocketed, reaching number one. But that was only the tip of the ice burg. There were many more such appearances. On talk shows, radio shows, and in debate halls, Jack excoriated what he called "The Christian Religious System" and with each appearance his book sales increased even more, until it seemed to be on its way to becoming the best-selling book of all time.

Things were not all sweetness and light for Jack, though. The trek through the seven cities had left their mark on him. On his back, specifically. He had two ruptured discs, and as time passed the pain grew worse and worse, until finally, he could endure no more, and admitted himself to the hospital for surgery. A friend of his had recommended a surgeon—Dr. Neeman—who was reputed to be the best in his field.

As he lay on the operating table, fast asleep, something remarkable happened. A man dressed in blue scrubs, with a long, flowing white beard, and a winsome glint in his eyes, entered the operating room entirely unnoticed by the medical team. He approached Jack, who lie on his stomach, his back split wide open. The man reached into Jack's back, felt around for a few moments, and then brought his hand back out. In it was one of Jack's ribs. He held it up to the light, examining it. Then he smiled and left the room, rib in hand.

The entire incident passed unnoticed by anyone, and the operation was a success. A week later, Jack visited Dr. Neeman for a follow up. As he sat there on the examining table, legs crossed at the ankles, he reflected on the last year. So much had happened so fast that it did not seem real. It was like a dream. So much so that he sometimes found himself wondering if it truly was real. But it was, of course. That much he knew for sure.

The doctor came in. "How are we feeling today?" he asked, gazing at Jack's chart. "Well," Jack replied, "I don't know how you're feeling, but I'm still sore."

The doctor laughed and started noodling around Jack's back, having him bend this way and that, and asking if it hurt. When he was finished, he said, "Looking good" and pronounced him to be on the road to recovery. Before leaving the doctor fished a card out of his pocket and handed it to

Jack, saying, "An associate of mine at the hospital gave me this. Told me to give it to you."

Jack looked at the card. The name on it was Evette Farber. She was a business consultant. He looked back at the doctor, who said, "He thought you might like this girl. Maybe you should give her a call."

"Maybe I will," Jack said.

But when he went home, Jack put the card on his dresser and forgot all about it. There was too much to do. By now he was in huge demand and he went on a speaking tour. He started in the U.S., and then worked his way to other countries, then other continents, until he had spoken in just about every major city in the world. The tour lasted a year, by which time the book had been made into a major motion picture and had sold more copies than any other book in history other than the Bible. And some were beginning to suggest, tongue in cheek, that it might one day surpass even that. Simply put, it was a singular phenomenon, unlike anything that had ever come before, launching Jack Horn so high into the stratosphere that he grew dizzy just thinking about it. Everyone wanted to see him, to talk to him, to have their picture taken with him, to touch him. The world was at his feet.

But through it all, he was lonely. Women threw themselves at him, but he threw them right back. He did not want women. He wanted one woman. He dated from time to time. But it never led anywhere. He was like a tiger roaming through a field full of celery: it was all right there for the taking, but he had no interest in it. He nibbled here and there, then moved on.

Then one day, while cleaning off his dresser, he noticed the card. There it was, staring at him, in the same place he had left in three weeks prior. He picked it up and stared at it. He decided to give it a try; after all, what did he have to lose? The worse that could come of it was another boring first date with someone he would never see again. He'd had plenty of those in the last two years; one more wouldn't kill him. So, he called the number. She answered on the second ring. A few minutes later, he had a date for Saturday night. They would be meeting at the Crab Shell, a nice restaurant in midtown Sacramento.

But first he had another date, with a very special lady—his mother. He would be taking the first plane to Tulsa in the morning. It would be only the second time since his father died that he would be seeing her. He had wanted to move her out to California to be near him, but she had stubbornly refused. She had her life, her church, her three sisters, and all her favorite places, there in Tulsa and she was not leaving. Maybe someday, when she was old and feeble, but not now. So, Jack figured, if the mountain wouldn't come to Mohammad . . .

⌒

The next day Jack was on the plane. By now flying was second nature to him. It wasn't much different than taking a walk to the corner store. The plane touched down at the Tulsa International Airport. Jack grabbed his bag and got off. As he touched ground, he began looking around, searching the crowd for his mom. Within seconds he spotted her—a short, thin, auburn haired woman, smiling ear to ear and holding up a sign that read *Adam*. Jack ran up to her and the two embraced. "You still need to gain some weight," Jack said. "I will tonight," she replied. "I'm making us enough food to feed a rugby team." On that note, they piled into Sara's white Ford Sedan and drove back to her home in midtown Tulsa.

Sara was good to her word about the meal she had prepared: turkey, with creamed corn, biscuits, three kinds of vegetables, and cranberry sauce, followed by apple pie, pastries, and soda. That was followed by coffee, which they took over to the sofa, where they talked.

"So, tell me," Sara said, "What's it like to be a big star?"

Jack thought about it for a moment and said, "It's great."

"Just great? That's it?"

"Well, what do you want me to say?"

"Come on, you're a writer. *Elaborate*."

Jack laughed. "I don't know. Truth is I've been too busy to really think about it. I think I'm still learning how to deal with it. I'm still trying to process the whole thing."

"It's a lot to process," Sara agreed.

"Yeah, it is."

"And what about your safety? Are people still . . ."

"Trying to kill me?" Jack said.

"Yes."

"Probably. But now I've got a lot of security. I should be all right."

"And what about you?" Jack asked. "How are you doing?"

Sara sighed. "It's been hard without your father; I won't lie. I miss him every day. But I'm so glad you made your peace with him before he left. He died with a smile on his face, and I think you played a big part of that."

"I'd like to think so," Jack said. For the rest of the evening they kept things on the lighter side, talking about movies and old friends, watching television, and playing around with Schnuckims and Pookey. Jack spent the night in his old room. The next morning, his mother drove him back to the airport. They parted with light hearts, each secure in the knowledge that the other was okay.

⟞

Jack had never been on a blind date before. He was nervous. He pulled into the lot of The Crab Shell, got out of his car, and headed for the entrance, playing with his hair as he walked along. He went inside. He had been there a few times before. It was nothing fancy: tables in the center, booths on raised platforms on the sides. Candles on the tables, paintings on the walls, a high ceiling with three chandeliers, one in each section of the restaurant. The lighting was dim, the atmosphere romantic. It was a good place to go on a date.

Jack approached the maitre d' and said, "I'm meeting someone here; her name's . . ." Jack realized he had forgotten the woman's name. He was so *stupid*. He slapped himself on the head. The maitre d, a dashing young man wearing a red and black uniform, just stared at him patiently, a slight smile on his handsome face. "Oh, I remember," Jack said, relieved, "Her name's Evette Farber. Did anyone by that name come in?"

"No, not yet," the man replied. "Okay," Jack said, eying his watch. It was a quarter to eight. He was a bit early. "I'll take a booth," he said. "Right this way, sir," the man said, leading him to a booth. "I'll bring her right over when she shows up."

"Thank you," Jack said as he slid into the booth. On the wall next to him was a painting, and next to that, a light fixture. On the thick, cherry colored table were two place settings. On the end of the table were salt and pepper shakers, and in the middle, a candle in a cylindrical glass holder.

As the minutes rolled by, Jack started to fidget, looking around. He started to wonder if she was going to show up. He looked at his watch; it was ten to eight. Only a few minutes had passed; it just *felt* longer.

A few minutes later he saw a woman heading for his table. She was wearing a long, black dress that accentuated a slim hour glass figure. Her black pumps clickety clacked as strolled gracefully along, placing one shoe directly in front of the other, like a runway model, and yet, somehow, there was nothing showy about it; her walk, her gait, her manner, were pure grace and elegance. Her dress was cinched at the waist with a white belt. Her long, flowing blond hair contrasted wonderfully with her black dress, and her blue eyes sparkled like pools of water. Jack was speechless as she stood before him, extending her hand. "Hi, I'm Evette," she said with a smile. Breathless, Jack stood up and shook her hand. It felt like silk. "I'm Jack," he said, smiling stupidly. He *felt* stupid. For the past two years he had not been moved much by the women he met, even though most of them were gorgeous, and he had pretty much forgotten that he still *could* experience that kind of a reaction.

Evette slid into the booth across from him. He just stared at her, dumbfounded. "Nice place," she said. "Yeah," Jack said simply. *Stupidly.* It was literally all he could think of to say. The neurons in his brain were simply not firing with sufficient force to enable him to form complex sentences. She gave him a bemused look, like a teacher might give to a confused kindergarten student. "Have you ever been here before?" she asked. "Oh, I'm sorry," Jack said, trying to snap himself out of it. "Yes, I have. Twice."

The waiter came over with the menus. He was a short, squat man, with thinning black hair and a small wart on his left cheek. "How are you folks doing this evening?" he asked. "Very well," Evette answered for the both of them. "Would you like any drinks?" he asked. "I'll have a scotch on the rocks," Evette said. Jack ordered a soda water. He had not touched drugs or alcohol for two years. "Very good," the waiter said, "I'll be back in a few minutes to take your orders." They thanked him as he sauntered off.

"So, what's good here?" Evette asked, opening the menu. "Let's see," Jack said, "Once I had the chicken marsala, and once I had the steak. They were both good."

The words were getting easier now; the neurons were doing their job. "Steak, hey?" Evette said, "I haven't had a good steak in ages. I'll go with that." Then she closed the menu. That was the fastest Jack had ever seen a woman decide on what to eat. "I think I'll have the same thing," Jack said, closing the menu. A few moments of silence passed, then Evette said, as if suddenly remembering something important, "I read your book." She opened her purse and took out a copy as Jack said, "Oh, really; did you like it?"

"I loved it," she said, holding up a copy and sliding it toward him, along with a pen. "Could you sign it for me?"

"Sure," Jack said. He scribbled something on the inside jacket and handed it back to her. She clutched it in her hands and said with a voice full of excitement, "Can I ask you something about it?"

"Sure," Jack said, trying his best not to sound as flattered as he felt.

"Was there really a Diane?" she asked.

"Yes, there was," Jack replied. Evette smiled shyly and said, "That was my favorite part. I love romance novels." Jokingly, she held the book to her chest and fluttered her eyelashes. Then she put a hand on his and asked, "Was all that stuff true? You know, where you say . . ." She opened the book to a page that had been folded over at the corner and read: Her job was to get you going. And she did. And in the process, she made you better. You're selfish, she's selfless; you're lazy, she's diligent; you're sloppy, she's meticulous; you're closed minded, she's open-minded. But now, you are better than when you started. More like her. And she's the reason. She is your other half.

With his hand tingling from her touch, Jack said "Yes, all of that stuff is true."

"Wow!" Evette exclaimed, "That's so . . . romantic." Her voice quivered when she said the last word. Then she put a hand to her throat and said "I'm sorry . . . I didn't mean to get so choked up."

And then she just sat there, holding Jack's hand, and staring deep into his eyes. Somehow, it did not feel the least bit awkward. In fact, it was the most comfortable Jack had felt for a long, long time. They sat like that for almost a minute. Then she said, "There's just one more thing. In the chapter on the city of the Snake People, you made a slight mistake."

"A mistake?" Jack asked curiously.

"Yeah," she said, leaning forward and speaking almost in a whisper. "You transposed the second halves of two names. You mentioned Crycon and Glycos. It was Crios and Glycon."

Jack stared at her in disbelief. There was only one person who could know that. And now, as he stared at her, there was a sudden spark of recognition. It was her. She looked different, but there was no mistaking it: it was her. He could see it in her eyes. "Diane," he whispered. "Uh huh," she said simply, and gave his hand a squeeze. "It's you. It's really you," he said. "How . . . how could it be? How did you come back?" Diane shrugged and said, "I think . . . someone decided that you needed me."

"They were right," Jack said, his eyes welling with tears. He ran over to her and threw his arms around her so tight he was afraid he might crush her. "I've missed you so much," he cried. "I know, I know," she said, caressing the back of his head with both of her hands. "I love you so much, Jack."

And for almost a minute, they stood like that, locked in a tight embrace, their eyes flowing with tears of joy. Then Jack withdrew, grabbed her by the shoulders and just stared at her, as if trying to comprehend that she was really there. As if reading his mind, she whispered "It's me."

"Yeah," he said, his voice hoarse, "It is, isn't it? It's really you." She cupped his chin with her hand and whispered, "And this time I'm not going anywhere." Her gently smiling face, wet with tears, was the most radiant thing Jack had ever seen. "You'd better not," Jack whispered. She just shook her head.

Jack sat back down and managed to compose himself. After several moments, he asked "So how about we get married right away and spend the rest of our lives together?"

"You think that would work?" she whispered, leaning forward until her lips were just inches from his. "I mean now that you're such a big shot."

"I think it might," Jack said. "Then let's try it," she cooed, and gave him a quick, soft peck on the lips. Jack could smell her perfume; he could taste her lipstick. It sent shivers through him. "Okay, we will," he said

"Then what?" she asked, giving him another peck, as she removed her shoe and ran her foot up his shin. "Then the honeymoon, I guess," Jack said. "And where should we go?" she asked, kissing him again. "How about Disneyland?" Jack offered. "That sounds great," Diane whispered, "I've always wanted to go to Disneyland." As she said the last word her lips touched his yet again. This time she kept them there for a good ten seconds. By the time she withdrew Jack felt like a mound of jello. "Disneyland, it is," Jack said, as the waiter arrived to take their orders. He never enjoyed a steak so much in his life.

23

Diane moved into Jack's apartment and they began planning their lives together. As for the wedding, they decided on a small one. Real small. Jack's only family was his mother and a few aunts that he hadn't seen for a decade. Diane had no family at all. Yes, Jack was a celebrity now and, had he wished, he could have packed any hall with thousands of acquaintances, but that's not the route he wanted to take. Instead they rented a small hall in Tulsa, and had a small, modest ceremony, attended only by family and a few friends. As for Diane's "resurrection", they told only Jack's mother, and Diane went by the name Evette, so as not to invite excessive media speculation. Neither wanted to turn their lives into a freak show. They just wanted a normal life together as husband and wife.

After the wedding, they honeymooned at Disneyland, as they had planned. Shortly after, they purchased a modest home in Sacramento, and began planning for the next chapter of their lives—parenthood. The following Christmas they were the proud parents of a bouncing baby boy. They named him Cain. He brought a whole new dimension of joy into their already blissful lives.

Absorbed as they were in their world of domestic bliss, they had not forgotten about their mission. Jack continued to maintain a busy schedule. He attended conferences, published essays, conducted workshops, and gave speeches throughout the world. An entire ministry sprang up around his message—TREE ministries—a collection of people devoted to sharing his vision with the world. It included a radio program, a powerful internet presence, a television show, and a slew of books and essays.

The movement grew into a crusade, and Jack began to fill up entire stadiums, with networks broadcasting his appearances live throughout the world. Whenever she could, Diane attended, cheering him on from the front row. But he also spoke at smaller venues, such as universities. One such appearance was at Sacramento City College, where he would be speaking about biblical hermeneutics, which was the study of how to properly interpret the Scriptures. Diane was there for the speech. She watched proudly from the front row as a male student wearing thick bifocals and wearing a cardigan sweater, introduced Jack by saying:

> "Our guest this evening shot into national prominence four years ago with the publication of a book called *The Tree Within*, a religious allegory about a couple's quest to lead the world back to the garden of Eden. Since then his journey of spiritual discovery has taken him around the world in a quest to promote a radically new way of interpreting the scriptures and understanding God. He is here tonight to share that vision with us. Ladies and gentlemen, let's have a very warm welcome for Jack Horn."

As Jack took the stage, Diane marveled at how he had grown over the years, from a shiftless kid who tried to shirk his calling into a mature, disciplined young man who embraced that calling with his whole heart, and did everything he could to live up the demands it placed on him.

He began by thanking the University, then launched into his speech. He spoke in his usual soft, almost subdued manner, without a lot of inflection or jokes; he didn't try to be cute or clever. And yet, somehow, he held the crowd's attention. The reason was simple: the message. He spoke what people felt; he struck a chord; he *resonated.*

About midway through the speech, two men in the front stood up, guns in hand. They pointed them at Jack and opened fire. Bedlam erupted as Jack fell backward. Security swarmed the stage, forming a circle around Jack. Other security men ran after the assailants, who ran for the exits. Hysterical, Diane rushed toward the stage, where she was restrained by the security team. Within minutes Jack was loaded onto a stretcher and taken by ambulance to Mercy General Hospital. Flanked by a caravan of police, Diane followed them in her car. She parked in the hospital lot and dashed over to the emergency room entrance, where she watched helplessly as the medics rushed her husband inside. She followed them in.

The hospital was buzzing with security people, police, and reporters. Diane demanded to know what was going on, but the hospital staff could only tell her to sit down and wait; they would keep her abreast of any new developments. For now, they could tell her only that Jack was alive, and they would do everything possible to save him. Two members of Jack's own security team took her by the arms and directed her over to a seat in the waiting room, where they sat with her. Sat and waited. As they waited, she looked up at the television in the corner of the room. A reporter was talking about the shooting, saying; *This just in. Famous author and speaker Jack Horn was shot while giving a speech at Sacramento City College. He was immediately taken to Mercy General hospital, where his condition is not known. There were two shooters; both have been apprehended. Nothing is known about them. We will give you more details as they become available to us.*

After thirty minutes a doctor came out and spoke with Diane. He told her that Jack had taken four bullets, two to the chest, one to the shoulder, and one to the head. He was in surgery, and they did not know if he would pull through. They would keep her abreast of any new developments.

In the meantime, Diane called Jack's mother and broke the news. Sara promised to be on the first plane to Sacramento.

Over the next two weeks some things changed, and some didn't. Jack survived the surgery. The bullets were removed from his body. His condition, however, was still critical; doctors still did not know if he would pull through. His mother arrived and stood with Diane at her home. They had also been permitted to see Jack, who drifted in and out of consciousness, and in and out of coherence. He was hooked up to an assortment of monitors and tubes.

Meanwhile, more news had dribbled out about the shooters. Apparently, they were just two disgruntled nut jobs—avid followers of Calvin Connors who believed something had to be done to stem the tide of heathenism that threatened to destroy our nation.

Each day Diane and Sara took turns keeping vigil at Jack's bedside. When one was there, the other was at home with Cain. One day, during Diane's "shift", Jack managed to summon up just enough strength to sustain a brief conversation. He began it by asking, in a barely audible voice, "How's Cain?"

"He's fine, honey," Diane said.

"Good," Jack replied. Then he stared into space for a moment, as if struggling to find his trend of thought, and said something that Diane could not hear. "Can you repeat that?" she said, leaning over, her ear only inches from his mouth. "Our mission," he said, using every ounce of his strength to speak. Diane looked at the monitors with concern. He was using up too much energy. "What about our mission, honey?" she asked.

"Did it succeed?" he asked. For a moment, she thought he had retreated to the past, really forgetting the past four years of his life. But she quickly realized that's not what had happened. He was there, in the present, with her. He had not forgotten the last four years; he just wanted to know if those years constituted success. She had wondered about that herself at times. But she wasn't about to tell him that. Not at this particular moment. So, she just said, "Of course it did. Of course, it succeeded."

As she spoke, she had one eye on him and another on the monitor that was recording his vital signs. And they weren't good. His blood pressure and heart rate were dropping. "Jack, I think you should rest now," she said.

"No," he said, "No. Let me speak."

"Okay," she said nervously.

"Take care of my mom," he whispered. With a terrible sense of dread, Diane realized that he was saying good bye. But that couldn't be. It wasn't time for good bye. They had their whole lives to spend together. "Your mom will be fine," Diane said, pushing the hair back from his forehead with one hand and holding his hand with the other. She felt like she should run for help now, but she couldn't. What if she left in the middle of his good bye and came back to find him dead?

He continued to speak, harking back to the mission again, but Diane was scarcely hearing the words, so obsessed was she with the monitor, which was showing a man on the precipice of death. That's when she felt him squeeze her hand so hard it hurt. "Listen to me!" he demanded in a quivering voice. "Yes, I am, dear! I am!" she said, her eyes welling with tears. This couldn't be happening. Not after all they had been through. It *couldn't* be ending like this.

Jack spoke with great effort, enunciating each word slowly and carefully "I don't know . . . if I led . . . anyone back to the garden. But I . . . found my own. It was you. You are my garden. When I'm with you, I am home."

And then he closed his eyes. "Jack?" she cried, looking frantically at the monitor as the lines started to flatten out. "Jack? Jack! Jack!!!" And then the line went straight, and a horrible beep filled the room. "No!" Diane cried, grabbing Jack's head in her hands and clutching it to her breast. "Get back here! Get back here!" she screamed as a medical team flooded into the room. They pried her off him and forced her out of the room as they attempted to revive him. She just stood there, weeping, as she looked at the door, until finally, a doctor came through it, and told her what she already knew: her husband was dead.

24

THE NEXT YEAR WAS the longest and most painful of Diane Foster's life. There were five stages to grief: denial, anger, bargaining, depression, and acceptance. For the first year after Jack's death, she found herself experiencing all four of the first five at the same time. There was denial: No, Jack wasn't really gone, any more than she was really gone the first time God had ripped the two of them apart. This was just another plot twist in the game God had been playing with them for the past five years. It was not permanent; a reversal was forthcoming, probably at a time she least expected it, and in some way that she could not anticipate. In due time God would employ yet another creative plot devise, like the ones used in soap operas and TV miniseries, to once again reunite the hero and heroine of this fanciful little story. Perhaps she had dreamed Jack's death; perhaps this was all part of *his* dream, or maybe they were all still back in one of the seven cities, stuck in their own thoughts, and would soon wake up, on the side of a road somewhere, to continue their mystical journey. That's what she told herself for a long time—as long as she could, until she could no longer make herself believe that it might be true.

There was anger: How dare God? How *dare* He! First, He sends her and Jack on a virtual rollercoaster of nightmarish torments. Then, he rips them apart, seemingly forever. Then, he finally throws them a bone, and reunites them. And then, in one final twist, he takes the bone back, and uses it to club Jack to death while she is forced to watch. Thanks Lord and *Fuck You!*

Then there was bargaining, which, in this case, was closely related to denial. Okay, God; can we come up with a better ending? How about you give me Jack back—use whatever plot device you want—and I go on national TV and tell the whole world how great you are? Or how about this: I will tell the world my true identity—that I'm not Evette Farber; I'm Diane

Foster, who *you brought back to life*. How about that? Wouldn't that be cool? Just give me Jack back and we can make it happen.

Then there was depression. Which for Diane took the form of a deep seeded feeling that every pain she had suffered, every trial encountered, every woe endured, from birth to the present day, was at best pointless, and at worst just fodder for the amusement of a God who saw us merely as playthings. Either she was the victim of blind indifference or cruel malevolence. Either way it sucked, and there was no reason for hope.

It was in this frame of mind that Sarah found her one evening, sitting alone by the fireplace, staring blankly at the floating embers. By this time, she had moved in with Diane, and the two had become quite close. "May I join you?" she asked, sitting next to her on the sofa. She held a copy of *The Tree Within* in her hands. "Of course," Diane said. She sat next to her, opened the book, and said "Do you mind if I read something to you?"

"Not at all."

She read the following words from chapter 18 of *The Tree Within*:

> "Well, think about it. Since when do people want to be shown the error of their ways? You think we're the first ones to try it? Anytime someone comes with a message like that, you know what people do? They kill them. Anyone who comes to people with a message of peace, a message of hope, a message of love; they kill them. John Kennedy came with that message. They killed him. Robert Kennedy came with that message. They killed him. John Lennon came with that message. They killed him. Mahatma Gandhi came with that message. They killed him. Martin Luther King came with that message. They killed him. Jesus Christ came with that message. They killed him. So, why should we be any different? People don't want to change. They don't want to think for themselves. And they don't want to love each other. And nobody's ever going to change that."

"You might be right, Jack," Diane said. "I don't know. But I didn't accept this mission because I wanted to change the world."

"Then why did you?"

"Because I was called."

Then Sara closed the book and said: "You said you accepted the mission because you were called."

"That's right," Diane said.

"Well, honey," Sara said, "the calling was never about you. You are called for others. To answer a calling, especially a calling like that, is, in a sense, to sacrifice yourself for those you are called to serve. And you might be called to sacrifice everything." Diane looked down at her knees.

"Why did Jack die?" Sara asked.

"Because his message made people mad," Diane answered.

"Exactly! He had to sacrifice his life for the message. And you had to sacrifice the joy of *being with him* for the message. You see it all as being senseless, but it's not. It makes perfect sense. It's part of the sacrifice you were called to make. Did you think the two of you would save the world and live happily ever after?"

"I . . . I guess I just wanted the happily ever after part."

"There is no happily ever after in this life, *especially* not for servants of God. There are two things, and only two, that God promises to people He calls. The first is *suffering,* and the second is the grace given, *as needed,* to endure it and carry on their mission. You accepted because you were *called.* Not because you thought you'd change the world. And guess what: you didn't. The world's the same as its always been. Just like it was after Gandhi left it. Just like it was after John Kennedy left it. Just like it was after Robert Kennedy left it. Just like it was after Martin Luther King left it. Just like it was after John Lennon left it. And just how it was after Jesus left it."

Diane looked at her strangely after those last words.

"That's right," she continued, "Jesus didn't make this world a better place. Hell, he didn't even try!" Sara whispered the next words in Diane's ear. "But that don't mean He didn't change it." She continued speaking in a normal tone. "He brought a message that touched the hearts and lives of millions. And, so did you and Jack. So, if you want to quit, then quit. You did what you were called to do. You can stop here if you want. You did your job. Fulfilled your calling. But don't stop because you think your mission failed. Don't stop because you didn't turn the world into a garden filled with birds and flowers and people loving each other everywhere you turn. And don't stop because you don't see the sense in the suffering God asked you to endure, because I'm here to tell you, as someone who just lost the man who meant everything to me *and* my son, that ain't no reason to stop. Stop if you want to stop. Stop if you're just too tired to go on. But otherwise—onward Christian soldier! And I will be right there with you every step of the way."

Diane looked down at her knees and whispered, in a voice filled with pain, "I don't know if I can do it without him."

"You're not supposed to know," Sara said. "But I'm ready to try if you are."

In the coming years Diane stepped out of the shadows and assumed a starring role in TREE ministries. She organized the finances, doled out the assignments, selected the personnel, and had a hand in managing all the affairs, great and small, that pertained to the ministry. She accepted every challenge, no matter how great, bore every burden, no matter how heavy, absorbed every blow, no matter how hard, and endured every hardship, no matter how cruel. And just as she promised, Sara was with her every step of the way.

And they changed the world, one heart at time, until a funny thing happened: the prophecy of Psalm 96:1—I will sing a new song—began to be fulfilled before there very eyes. Everywhere people turned—on TV, over the radio, on the internet, on billboards, in tracts, and, increasingly, even in pulpits—the new song was heard. And the new song was:

"God is love". (1 John 4:8)

"Love Worketh no ill". (Rom. 13:10)

"For God so loved the world that he gave his only begotten Son" (John 3:16),

"Have we not ALL one Father? Hath not one God created us?" (Mal. 2:10)

"Behold all souls are mine," saith the Lord "As the soul of the father, so also the soul of the son is mine." (Ezek. 18:4)

"The Father loveth the Son, and hath given all things into his hand." (John 3:35)

For this is good and acceptable in the sight of God our Saviour; Who will have all men to be saved, and to come unto the knowledge of the truth." (1 Tim. 2:4)

"Thy will be done." (Matt. 6:10)

"Thou hast created all things, and for thy pleasure they are and were created". (Rev. 4:11

"As I live, saith the Lord God, I have no pleasure in the death of the wicked". (Ezek. 33:11)

"Having made known unto us the mystery of his will, according to his good pleasure, which he hath purposed in Himself, that in the dispensation of the fullness of times, he might gather together in one all things in Christ, both which are in heaven, and which are on earth, even in him". (Eph. 1:9-10)

"In thee shall all the families of the earth be blessed". (Gen. 12:3)

"In thy seed shall all the nations of the earth be blessed". (Gen. 22:18)

"I have sworn by myself, the word is gone out of my mouth in righteousness, and shall not return, that unto me every knee shall bow, every tongue shall swear, surely shall say, in the Lord have I righteousness and strength." (Isaiah 45:23-24)

"He gave himself a ransom for all, to be testified in due time." (1 Tim. 2:6)

"But we see Jesus, who was made a little lower than the angels, for the suffering of death, crowned with glory and honor; that he, by the grace of God, should taste death for every man." (Heb. 2:9)

"And he is the propitiation for our sins; and not for ours only, but also for the sins of the whole world." (1 John 2:2)

"Behold, I bring you good tidings of great joy, which shall be to all people." (Luke 2:10)

"All nations whom thou hast made shall come and worship before thee, O lord, and shall glorify thy name." (Psalms 86:9)

"The Lord is good to all, and his tender mercies are over all His works." (Psalms 145:9)

"All thy works shall praise thee, O Lord, and thy saints shall bless thee." (Psalms 145:10)

"The Lord is merciful and gracious, slow to anger, and plenteous in mercy. He will not always chide; neither will He keep His anger forever." (Psalms 103:8-9)

"God will destroy, in this mountain, the face of the covering cast over all people, and the veil, that is spread over all nations." (Isaiah 25:7)

"God will swallow up death in victory." (Isaiah 25:8)

"The Lord God will wipe away tears from off all faces" (Isaiah 25:8)

"the glory of the Lord shall be revealed, and all flesh shall see it together." (Isaiah 40:5)

"I will not contend forever, neither will I be always wroth; for the spirit should fail before men, and the souls which I have made." (Isaiah 57:16)

"He retaineth not his anger forever, because he delighteth in mercy." (Micah 7:18)

"As, by the offence of one, judgment came upon all men to condemnation; even so by the righteousness of one, the free gift came upon all men unto justification of life." (Rom. 5:18)

"For the creation was made subject to vanity, not willingly, but by reason of him who subjected it; in hope that the creation itself also shall be delivered from the bondage of corruption, into the glorious liberty of the sons of God." (Romans 8:20)

"As in Adam all die, even so in Christ shall all be made alive". (1 Cor. 15:22) "he was given a name which is above every name, that at the name of Jesus every knee should bow, of things in heaven, and things in earth, and things under the earth; and that every tongue should confess that Jesus Christ is Lord, to the glory of God the Father." (Philip. 2:9-11)

"if we confess with the mouth the Lord Jesus, and believe in the heart that God hath raised him from the dead, we shall be saved." (Rom. 10:9

"No-one can say that Jesus is Lord, except by the Holy Ghost." (1 Cor. 12:3)

"And every creature which is in heaven, and on the earth, and under the earth, and such as are in the sea, and all that are in them, heard I saying, Blessing, and honor, and glory, and power, be unto him that sitteth upon the throne, and unto the Lamb, forever and ever". (Rev. 5:13)

"the tabernacle of God is with men, and he will dwell with them, and they shall be his people, and God himself shall be with them, and be their God". (Rev. 21:3)

"God shall wipe away all tears from their eyes; and there shall be no more death, neither sorrow, nor crying; neither shall there be any more pain; for the former things are passed away." (Rev. 21:4)

"For it pleased the Father that in him should all fullness dwell; And, having made peace through the blood of his cross, by him to reconcile all things unto himself; by him, I say, whether they be things in earth, or things in heaven." (Co. 1:19-20)

"Forasmuch then as the children are partakers of flesh and blood, he also himself likewise took part of the same; that through death he might destroy him that had the power of death, that is, the devil;" (Heb. 2:14)

"For this purpose, the Son of God was manifested, that he might destroy the works of the devil". (1 John 3:8)

"All things shall be subdued unto Christ,—Christ shall be subject unto Him that put all things under Him, that God may be all in all." (1 Cor. 15:28)

"Woe unto you, Scribes and Pharisees, hypocrites! for ye shut up the kingdom of heaven against men; for ye neither go in yourselves, neither suffer ye them that are entering to go in." (Matt. 23:13)

And as Diane's hair turned grey and her legs grew weak, that song sustained her, and gave her strength. And it always made her think of Jack, and whenever she did, she smiled.

www.ingramcontent.com/pod-product-compliance
Lightning Source LLC
Chambersburg PA
CBHW051140020726
47501CB00005B/1605